For my lovely friends
Jan and Bill
with my love
Jane x
x

Banzai's
Unexpected Voyage

By Jane-Anne Hodgson
Illustrations by Sam Hodgson

Whistling Cat Books

Banzai's Unexpected Voyage

Published by Whistling Cat Books
www.whistlingcatbooks.com

PO Box 385, Burford, OX18 9DH

Hardback ISBN 978-1-908607-04-1
Paperback ISBN 978-1-908607-05-8

Designed and typeset by HL Studios, Witney, Oxfordshire.

Printed and bound by Berforts Information Press Limited, Eynsham, Oxfordshire.

FSC
www.fsc.org
MIX
Paper from
responsible sources
FSC® C013262

For my Mum

Who taught me how to read and gave me her love of books, explained the importance of keeping life's baggage light and who sees the silver lining on the cloudiest of days.

Captain John Selby

In the book, it is Captain John Selby who tells the story, as it was recounted by all aboard The Beagle and The Resolve when they returned from their unexpected voyages.

The real Captain Selby was one of Jane's ancestors and he was a pirate – a good pirate! Registered to Elizabeth I, he was licensed to attack and raid the Spanish Armada.

Jane-Anne Hodgson

A former English teacher, Jane lives in Oxfordshire but she often runs away to Pembrokeshire where she spent many summers as a child and where she now writes.

The sea, the old harbour towns, hidden beaches and remote islands remain magical to her.

Banzai's Unexpected Voyage is the sequel to her first children's book, Grubson Pug's Christmas Voyage.

Sammy Jim!

More properly known as Sam Hodgson, he is Jane's oldest nephew. Sam and his brothers spent many childhood hours spinning tales of adventure and magic with their aunt. Now an art student, Sam was the natural choice as illustrator for these books. The illustrations in this book are all hand-drawn using pen and ink, which gives them a traditional feel.

Some pronunciations

Grubson is part French so his family all have French names, and the voyages take the crews of The Beagle and The Resolve to different countries across Europe. This means that you may need a bit of help to pronounce some names and words. I hope this helps.

Banzai	BANZ – eye
Bonsai	BONS – eye
Celeste	Sell – EST
Ciao	Chi-ow
Doge	DOE – j
Fabrice	fuh – BREECE
Guillaume	GEE – yom
Henri	on – REE
Jacques	zh-ack

Banzai's Unexpected Voyage

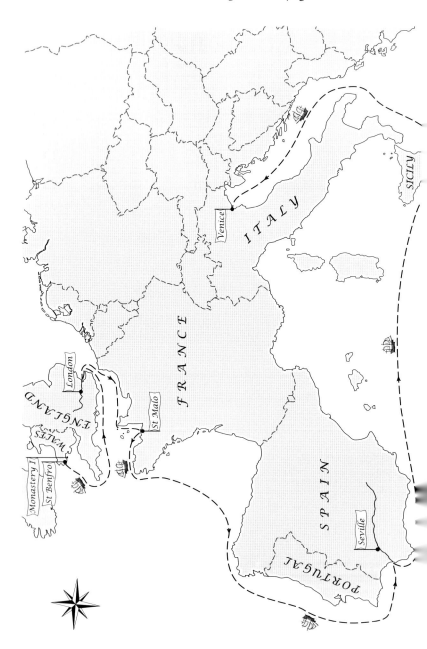

Contents

Foreword

*C*an you actually see a cat vanish?

A lot of people claim to have seen Banzai leave St Benfro on that snowy January morning – but that's not quite the same.

Horatio's Talking Telescope also watched him go and that's how Horatio Fox knew where he had gone. Others followed soon afterwards and they were all away for many weeks. None of us back in St Benfro heard anything from them for a long time. So when the ships and the sailors returned home, there was a great celebration in The Three Buccaneers.

The tiny old pub was crammed full that night – everyone wanted to know where they had been and what had happened.

We all listened as one by one, each of the sailors took a turn to tell their part of the story.

It's quite a strange story – no one would have guessed why Banzai had vanished or where he had gone or what would happen when he got there. But that's quite typical of Banzai – you have to expect the unexpected with him.

I pieced together everyone's stories and wrote this complete version. This is my story of what happened when Banzai vanished from St Benfro on his unexpected voyage. And I know you like him, so I thought you'd like to hear it.

Captain J. Selby

Banzai's Unexpected Voyage

Chapter One

Resolutions

The winter storms continued on and off over Christmas and into the New Year. The voyage home on Christmas Eve had almost ended on the rocks off Monastery Island, but Grubson had managed to save The Beagle and her crew by using all the Christmas presents he had travelled so far to find. A grand piano for Clementina, hand-made party dresses for Bella and a beautiful racing bicycle for his eldest son Fabrice. Only Henri, his youngest and most thoughtful child had not demanded a present.

Grubson felt sad that all of the gifts had been lost in the storm. Yet as it turned out, none of his children had complained. They were just very relieved to have him home safely. Perhaps they had learned something about Christmas after all. It wasn't all about children and presents as they had thought. It was about family and friends and looking after one another.

The shipwrights worked when the weather allowed: patching up the hole in the hold where the rocks had broken through. Clementina's grand piano had held firm like a giant plug, just long enough to return to harbour in St Benfro. Now it was nothing more than a heap of splintered wood and piano keys.

The sail-makers were stitching huge new canvas sheets to replace the tattered shreds which had been abandoned overboard during the storm. Bella's sequinned party dresses had been hoisted as emergency sails and were now being used as lacy cloths for cleaning and polishing the ship's brasses.

The remains of Fabrice's racing bike were rusting quietly on top of the piano pile. The bent wheels, which had been used to steer the ship into harbour, were being replaced by a beautiful new oak helm.

Marjorie, Grubson's trusted parrot, was busy on board The Beagle. She was overseeing the repairs. Marjorie liked to be in charge and was tireless as she hopped around the decks, flew up the masts and waddled below to the hold. She seemed to be everywhere at once – always looking over someone's shoulder to point out a bit of varnishing they may have missed, or a rope with a loose knot. The workmen did their best to see her as helpful, but couldn't help muttering under their breath as she had another little peck at something she felt could be improved.

Meanwhile the rest of the crew were bored. Sebastian and Lefty were half-heartedly collecting fat squishy sea-bloated oranges which were rolling onto the beach with the tide: the inedible remnants of the Spanish hamper they had bought for Christmas treats. They had nothing to do whilst The Beagle was being repaired and were desperate to get back to sea. Grubson suggested that they should take shore-leave for a few days. Sebastian went back to Barafundle to visit his family – now that Cecilia Savilton was safely out of the way there was no risk of being suddenly married off to her. Lefty went to Carew where he knew one of the wolfhounds at the castle (who had a sister he rather liked).

This left Banzai. The ship's cat who was famed for his arm-wrestling prowess, avoided for his garlic chewing habits and who constantly whistled sea-shanties and cheerful little tunes he liked to compose. Banzai, who was full of mischief and had nowhere to go and nothing to do. This was not a good state of affairs. He couldn't help himself – he kept getting in everyone's way and was generally annoying with his whistling and garlic-chewing habits. He kept interrupting the workmen on board the ship – challenging them to arm-wrestling fights or leaving his huge carpet bag where it would be tripped over. Rather than lose the workmen, Grubson had ordered his cat off the ship and had Banzai to stay with him and his family until the work was finished.

After breakfast on the sixth of January, Grubson gathered his wife Adele, his children and Banzai around the long kitchen table. After a good deal of scrambling and shuffling and settling onto stools Grubson announced,

"The New Year is well under way now and after all the excitement and events around Christmas, it is time to make our resolutions."

Six pairs of eyes blinked at him and no one said anything.

"I think we all know what we have to do," Grubson continued, "but it might be a good idea to make a big list of resolutions. We can pin it on the wall so that we can see them every day and be reminded of what we intend to do this year."

There was a bit of puffing and sighing around the table, even some tutting and somebody hummed, but Grubson couldn't quite tell who was doing what.

Grubson unfurled a big scroll of paper and spread it on the table, weighted at the corners with large pebbles. He smiled at his eldest child as he passed her the fat pen. Clementina said nothing but stretched as far as she could reach and wrote in big letters:

PRACTISE MY SCALES AND ARPEGGIOS EVERY DAY – CLEMENTINA

Grubson nodded approvingly. Fraulein Schneerer had been passionate in her explanation of how much work Clementina would need to do if she was to become a concert pianist.

"I know what I have to do Papa," said Clementina. "And so do you Bella!" handing the pen to her sister.

Bella immediately scowled, but then somehow turned it into a pretend sneeze before giving everyone her best and most dazzling smile.

"Thank you, Clementina," she said insincerely and taking the pen, she hovered over the scroll of paper.

"Well?" asked Grubson kindly. "Do you know what you should do to make your dreams come true?"

"Yes," said Bella. "It's just – difficult."

"That's where you might be wrong," said Grubson. "I know you want to be thought of as pretty –"

"Beautiful!" corrected Bella.

"And to be loved by all your friends," continued Grubson.

"Adored by everyone!" interrupted Bella again.

"Well these are big ambitions," said Grubson in a fatherly way. "And I want you to know that you have never looked prettier to me than when I returned from the stormy voyage. You were soaking wet and your fur was clumpy, your bow was flattened but you were smiling and happy. You had forgotten to show off – you weren't just thinking about yourself. This is exactly what Senor Castanet said makes someone beautiful – inside as well as outside."

Bella stared into Grubson's eyes and then wrote:

BE KIND TO MY FRIENDS AND STOP SCOWLING AND SHOWING OFF AND BEING JEALOUS – BELLA

Fabrice leaned over and took the pen from Bella. He knew what had to be done and in fact he had already decided that as soon as the Christmas pudding, Christmas cake, mince pies and special sweetie treats were gone, he'd start! (Although Easter wasn't far away and that meant lots of chocolatey eggs and more cakes.)

Slurping at a huge treacly toffee, he tried not to dribble as he leant over the scroll and wrote:

STOP SNACKING AND EATING SWEETIES AND TRAIN EVERY DAY ON MY BICYCLE – FABRICE

Fabrice was not exactly built for speed, unlike Frankie Aquitaine, the whippet who had explained the dedication needed to become a champion cyclist. Grubson watched his son carefully and suggested that he make that toffee last, as it should really be, the last.

There was a sudden scrambling as Henri jumped up onto the table, whisked the pen from Fabrice's paw and turned to his father, brandishing the pen.

"Papa – I don't have a message from a shopkeeper but I do have a resolution. I know exactly what I want to do and how to do it. I've been learning about seafaring and charts and navigating and I know I'm ready. This year I want to make my first voyage on The Beagle – with you. Please." He was wheezing slightly.

In the past Henri had been laughed at by his older brother for being so small and weak. His mother and sisters had always ignored his ambitions to be a sailor, scoffing at the big dreams of a tiny dog. But everyone knew how much he wanted this and he had proved his commitment during the storm. Henri wrote on the scroll:

MAKE A VOYAGE ON THE BEAGLE – HENRI

Grubson smiled. He was quietly very proud of his youngest, tiniest, son.

"Now then – pass the pen on to Banzai… Where's Banzai?"

Seeing the pen coming closer to him round the table, Banzai had silently slunk off his stool and was now backing away. Eyeing the pen nervously he lifted his carpet bag, heaved it over his shoulder and started to speak very fast.

"I've just remembered somewhere I've got to be – someone I have to see – I have to see a dog about a cat,

I mean a cat about a dog – thank you all so much but I really must be …"

"Banzai?" said Grubson. But he was met only by an icy blast of January air rushing into the house and the sound of the front door closing.

Chapter Two

Banzai's Boredom

Alone in the house the following afternoon, Banzai was even getting on his own nerves. He stopped whistling. Then he suddenly became very aware of the stink of garlic which surrounded him. He spat out the chewy bits in his mouth and sucked on a lemon to sweeten his breath. This caught him by surprise and shrivelled his tongue, forcing him to suck in his cheeks and made his eyes water.

He was so fed up.

He wandered upstairs, trailing his tail behind him, scuffing his feet along the landings as he peered at family portraits of Grubson ancestors – Welsh and French, they were nearly all sailors and one of them looked very much like a pirate. Shoulders slumped and ears flattened, Banzai flumped heavily back downstairs and dawdled into the kitchen. He stared at the big scroll of resolutions.

Empty of everyone, the house was frozen into silence. Apart from the big old grandfather clock which steadily ticked and tocked, counting off the minutes for anyone who was bored enough to listen. Banzai circled the huge kitchen table in time to the clock – slowly and stiffly stepping like a clockwork cat. After eight laps of the table he was shaken out of his mechanical trance by the chiming of mid-day. Twelve booming notes echoed into the silence and made his tail spike out like a bottle-brush. He hated it when it did that.

"That's enough Banzai!" he spoke sternly to himself. Stroking his tail fur smooth again, he stood in front of the resolutions and knew what he had to do. He just couldn't face it. He dragged his big carpet bag from behind Clementina's old piano where he had hidden it and springing out a claw, he picked at the grime which was lodged in the silver clasp. He knew he wanted to be free of his bag. All these years he'd carried it everywhere and he'd kept the contents a big secret. Now he needed to empty it and be free. It was too big and heavy for one small cat to carry – no matter how strong he was.

The front door clattered open as Adele Grubson and all four of her children returned home. They were pleased to see Banzai back in the house, but had been warned not to ask questions about where he had been and who he'd been to see or who the cat was who knew about a dog. Henri ran over to him waving two letters which he had just collected from the postman.

"Look Banzai!" he exclaimed excitedly. "A letter for you from Siam – look at the stamp!"

"Another one," said Banzai gloomily. Taking it from Henri he stuffed it, unopened, into his carpet bag and sighed. "What's the other one?"

Henri bubbled with excitement, "It's an invitation from my good friend Horatio Fox for you and me to go to Gunfort Mansions for tea. If we go now we should just be in time!"

Banzai pulled himself together – he knew he was behaving badly and making everyone feel sad. This wasn't good old Banzai at all and this little pup was doing his best to cheer him up.

"Righty-O Henri," he said brightly. "Just give me a moment to put on my best bandana and I'll be right with you." He nosed about inside his bag, extracted his special-occasion bandana and, having tied it securely onto his head, he heaved his heavy old bag over his shoulder once again and secured it to his leg with a chain.

Five minutes later, Henri and Banzai set off along the harbour wall towards the town and Gunfort Mansions, breathing in big salty gusts of fresh sea air – how they both wished to be out on the sea sailing off on a voyage to adventure. Banzai was much happier now that he was out of the house and Henri trotted by his side explaining all about Horatio's wonderful turreted flat on the roof of the tallest building in St Benfro.

Horatio Fox was Henri's best friend. He studied the sea and astronomy and read Latin books and wrote letters to professors. He had inherited the flat and all the booty collected by his pirate aunt: telescopes, Chinese rugs, huge oil paintings, ivory carvings, pearl necklaces, a monkey skull, gold and silver by the chest load, maps and maritime charts, clocks and jewels – and that was only what Henri had seen. Horatio's aunt had been a very busy pirate! Banzai thought he would like to have known her.

Henri was wheezing by the time they had climbed eight flights of stairs to reach the top flat. And so was Banzai – he was very strong from kickboxing and had good bicep muscles from arm-wrestling, but it was pure determination which got that huge weighty bag all the way up there. Standing outside Horatio's front door, Banzai licked his paws and smoothed away the beads of sweat from his nose and ears before tugging the bell-pull. The door immediately opened to reveal the kindly and bespectacled face of Horatio Fox.

Banzai refused Horatio's offer to carry his bag inside for him but it seemed even heavier to him as he lugged it through the doorway, down the hall and into Horatio's drawing room. It was almost immoveable by the time he dumped it down in the middle of a beautiful Chinese rug and he was panting loudly as he bent double, hands on hips, trying to get his breath back.

Horatio was too polite to ask what was inside the bag, but he raised an eyebrow enquiringly as Banzai straightened up and puffed.

"Just – a few – essentials," he panted as he forced a smile across his face. "If it's all right with you sir, I'll just leave it exactly there – right there in the middle of the rug – in the middle of the room. Not in your way I hope? But I just don't seem to have the strength . . ." his voice trailed away.

Stooping down again, Banzai unclipped the silver chain which secured his bag to his foot.

"That's better I'm sure?" said Horatio kindly. "Now please make yourselves comfortable whilst I bring in the tea and a freshly baked ginger cake."

By the time he reappeared with a silver tea tray, Horatio found Henri and Banzai peering into the cabinets full of ancient and foreign artefacts and staring up at the huge oil paintings of galleons on stormy moonlit seas. Horatio's flat was a treasure trove of interesting and unusual objects. There were lots of things to ask about and every time Banzai thought he had seen everything in the room, he noticed something else. This kept them talking a long time as Horatio explained his nautical instruments and astronomy charts and told them about the book he was writing.

Eventually silence descended and all three found themselves staring at the only object in the room which hadn't been explained. Banzai's bag.

Banzai knew what was coming. There was something about Horatio Fox which meant that, sooner or later, you knew you would have to answer questions and he'd know if you were telling the truth.

Horatio opened the conversation.

"Banzai. Might I ask what it is that you keep in your heavy carpet bag? It is obviously very important to you. However, I have to say that it seems to be a burdensome weight and it must be hard to spend your life chained to it," said Horatio gently.

"IT is chained to ME," said Banzai slightly rudely – he didn't enjoy being questioned.

Horatio was undeterred.

"Well to me – to anyone looking at you – it seems that YOU are chained to IT, Banzai," said Horatio firmly. "What a terrible burden to carry. It must make you tired and weary. Perhaps even a bit depressed with such a weight on your shoulders."

Banzai, for once, said nothing. But he nodded.

"I've seen this kind of thing happen to people before – mainly cats, admittedly. You need a hand to empty that bag and be free of it! Perhaps Henri and I could help?"

Henri and Horatio watched as Banzai spontaneously broke into beads of sweat on his nose and ears again. Even thinking about the contents of his bag seemed to drag him down and put him under pressure. And thinking about opening it – and emptying it – with other people!

There then followed a stream of fast talking as Banzai tried to explain why he couldn't possibly open the bag.

"The lock's jammed . . . Is that the time? I've got to be off . . . Too much stuff inside. Once it's out, I might not be able to fit it all back in . . . It will be smelly. Garlic. Terrible, awful, garlic smells which will make Horatio possibly pass out . . ."

Eventually Banzai ran out of 'reasons' not to open the bag and blurted, "I'd love to be free of this weight I carry. I'm just afraid that my bag contains some very difficult problems and worries. Troubles and secrets which I have never been able to leave behind. Anywhere. I carry them everywhere. But it's getting me down and making me unhappy and I would love to be free." Banzai's voice was getting stronger as he spoke.

Henri patted Banzai's knee in a comforting way as Horatio smiled and said, "Then let's set to it, Banzai! I will clear away the tea tray and then I suggest you empty out your bag – right here on the Chinese rug. And I mean empty it – every last bit!"

Chapter Three

The Bag Gives Up
Its Secrets

anzai was whistling nervously as he unlocked
his carpet bag and cranked it open – a little way.
Trying to appear more confident than he felt, he
poked his head into the darkness within and nosed about.
Still keeping up his tuneless whistling.

Henri and Horatio glanced at each other. The longer
Banzai scratted about inside the bag, the more nervous

Henri, and the more concerned Horatio, became. They didn't know what to expect but Banzai's secrecy and reluctance to open the bag had made them brace themselves for something worrying or possibly unnerving and quite likely very frightening.

Neither of them had expected a teddy!

It was not so much a teddy bear – more of a teddy cat. Banzai whipped the little white knitted cat out of his bag in a big flourish and waved it about above his head. A thousand speckles of silver glittered through the air.

"This is Mr.Wong!" he exclaimed. "All the knittens in my family are called Mr.Wong. He has travelled all over the world with me on many voyages. My grandmothers knitted him for me when I was born. "

Perhaps I should explain something about baby Siamese cats which you may not know. When they are born, the grandmother cats get together and start knitting. Fast. They have to knit quickly because each of the kittens in a litter needs a knitted kitten – a knitten. The Siamese kittens cuddle their knittens whilst they are tiny and keep them all of their lives as constant companions. The grandmother cats use special wool and knit in a very particular way as each knitten must closely resemble the kitten who owns it.

Banzai's knitten was white (like Banzai) and had a greyish nose, ears, paws and tail (like Banzai) which sparkled and glittered in the light (not like Banzai who did not sparkle and glitter in the light, or anywhere else for that matter). Each knitten's sparkly nose gives its owner a sensitive sense of smell. Every knitten has glittery ears to give its kitten sharp hearing. All four knitten paws must always sparkle with the magical thread to give a kitten fast feet and no knitten would be without a twinkly tail – which helps kittens to balance in tricky situations.

As the kittens get older and become fully grown cats, they keep their knittens somewhere safe to bring them luck. They *are like magical mascots and most Siamese cats are very superstitious about their personal knittens – never travelling anywhere without them.*

Banzai stopped waving his knitten about in the air and stroked him gently, looking lovingly into his blue eyes (like Banzai's) which also sparkled (like Banzai's).

Henri was entranced by the beautiful little knitted cat.

"Mr.Wong is very lovely, Banzai," he sighed, hoping Banzai would offer his knitten for a cuddle.

"But he must weigh very little," observed Horatio Fox. "He's very small and very light and I can't see what kind of problem he might cause you?"

Banzai kissed Mr.Wong on the nose (which made his lips all glittery) and sighed.

"He doesn't cause me any problems at all. He is my friend through thick and thin. He helps me be a very excellent Siamese cat because of the sparkles he has. I suppose I would be embarrassed for any of the crew to know that I have him – because they think I am very tough and brave – and I AM very tough and brave. But I wouldn't want to be without my knitten. And they probably wouldn't understand – because they're not cats," explained Banzai.

"You might be surprised," smiled Horatio. "Sailors are famously very superstitious. It's probably because they have to be very brave to face stormy seas and pirates and all the dangers which may wait for them at sea. They need to feel they might have a bit of luck on their side. And anyway, we know that your knitten brings you more than luck. He brings you your marvellous cat talents."

Banzai smiled as he wondered what lucky mascots Lefty, Sebastian, and even Marjorie, might have stowed away on The Beagle. And what about Captain Grubson? Maybe Banzai himself was Grubson's lucky mascot – after all, he never liked to set sail without his ship's cat on board.

Feeling better now that Mr.Wong was out in the open, Banzai once again creaked open his carpet bag. A number of items came out in quick succession.

A slightly frayed bandana – he was wearing his special-occasion best bandana.

A pair of silk pyjamas – "Never been worn. Just in case."

"In case of what?"

"Just in case."

Several bulbs of fresh garlic. Banzai's favourite chewy treat to help him concentrate, calm him down – and keep vampires away. Just in case.

A beautiful brass telescope, which had been hand-made and carefully balanced to suit a cat. He had won this from another ship's cat in Valparaiso, but that was another story.

By the time these had come out of the bag and were arranged on the Chinese rug alongside Mr.Wong, Horatio was wondering what all the fuss was about. After all, there was nothing terrible here. And what could be so heavy – weighing down the bag like that?

Banzai stood up straight, stretched his arms above his head and flexed his biceps. He leaned down into the bag once more and proudly brought out three bulging money bags. Each bag was filled to bursting with gold and silver coins.

"Now these must weigh a lot," surmised Horatio. "But again, I can't see all this money as being a problem to you?"

Banzai explained that the money had been won in harbour bars all over the world where he had spent his evenings arm-wrestling salty sailor dogs. They always underestimated the cheeky little cat because he looked a bit weedy – but he was in fact very strong and his arm-wrestling technique had been finely tuned. He never lost.

However, he didn't know what to do with the money because he lived on The Beagle and Captain Grubson provided his food and drink. Banzai hardly ever bought new clothes and he already owned everything he needed. So he just kept all the money in his carpet bag and lugged it around with him.

Henri spent a happy hour counting out all the money and stacking the coins into tottering towers on Horatio's desk. It was a small fortune. Horatio congratulated Banzai for not wasting it but advised him that perhaps he should save some of it somewhere safe – just in case.

"In case of what?"

"Just in case."

Whilst Henri was counting out the money, Banzai and Horatio decided that perhaps some should be saved and some should be spent on something good or helpful for someone else. Banzai sat and stroked his knitten for a long time, thinking hard about how his money could be put to good use.

He finally made up his mind and without saying a word, he heaved two of the money bags into Horatio's safe which was hidden in the wall behind a portrait of his pirate aunt. The third money bag stayed out ready to go back into the carpet bag for him to put to good use.

The bag now weighed a lot less than it had before, but Banzai still seemed to struggle with it as he moved it from the Chinese rug onto a low leather footstool. Horatio's eyes narrowed as he asked what was next.

"Well . . .," said Banzai quietly. "It's nothing really. Probably not worth bothering with. Except that it does worry me."

Horatio said nothing and Henri tried not to wheeze too loudly – Banzai's reluctance was making him nervous again.

Disappearing back into the bag once more, Banzai reappeared with a huge sheaf of letters. Dozens and dozens of tissue-paper letters wafted out of his arms and fluttered across the room, slipping underneath chairs and hovering in the warm air near the fireplace. Some of the letters were opened and many more were still sealed. Henri recognised the stamps and the writing – all from the same person in Siam.

Although the letters were written on tissue thin paper and each one probably weighed less than a feather, the bundle seemed to be very heavy to Banzai. The strong little cat puffed with the effort as he caught the stray letters and tried to hold them all in his arms.

It might be useful at this point to tell you that Banzai had a past. He was not proud of it. His shameful secret was that he had not tried at school. At all. He hadn't learned how to read or write saying that sums and books were just BORING. On days when he was supposed to be in school he was catching fish in the river or kickboxing and arm-wrestling with older cats. His mother had begged him to pay attention at school and spent many hours trying to teach him to read at home, but he would never sit still long enough to learn. He just thought school was a big waste of a kitten's time.

As soon as he could, he naughtily ran away. Leaving his home in the middle of the night when everyone was sleeping, he followed the river to the sea. He left Siam by stowing away on board different ships and earned his keep through arm-wrestling. Eventually he was found in a bar by Grubson Pug and joined the crew of The Beagle, where he became an excellent ship's cat.

He knew all the tissue-paper letters were from his mother but because he couldn't read, he didn't know what she had written. He was too ashamed to ask for help from Grubson or the crew. So the letters piled up inside his bag and the guilt and shame got bigger and heavier. Now Banzai was concerned that perhaps his mother thought he didn't care about her or maybe she thought he was just very rude. Or possibly she was anxious that he might have been lost at sea. Yet he had never written her a letter. His eyes filled with tears every time he pictured her worried face.

Henri was bewildered by Banzai's problem. He felt very sorry for him because not only was Banzai very guilty and worried about his mother, but he could never enjoy reading a story-book or even understand important notices. He suddenly remembered Banzai's face as he had backed out of the kitchen when they were writing resolutions and understood why he had mysteriously run off into the night. He couldn't write.

Henri and Banzai looked at Horatio, hoping for some help. He was chewing on the stalk of an unlit pipe. He never smoked it – he was too young for that, but it helped him to think. After a little bit of pipe chewing and an examination through the window of one of his artefact cabinets, Horatio seemed to reach a decision. He unfurrowed his brow and said that he had a solution to Banzai's problem, but before explaining it he wanted Banzai to finish emptying the carpet bag. The great opening had taken quite some time and he suspected that bigger problems still lay within.

"How does your bag feel now Banzai?" he asked. "It looks almost empty. Perhaps it could be moved off the footstool now and I can put my feet up?"

"Oh I think it will be fine now, thank you Horatio," answered Banzai without looking at him. "I don't think you need to help me anymore. I'm very grateful. Thank you." He was nervously stroking Mr.Wong's tail as he spoke, hugging him for comfort.

Henri hopped down off the velvet sofa and picked up the bag.

"I can move it," he said helpfully. "Where shall I put it?"

The little pug easily lifted the big old bag and swung it from side to side to demonstrate how light it now was.

In a cloud of glittering speckles, the knitten was launched through the air as Banzai leapt into action and whisked the bag out of Henri's paws. He immediately dropped it to the floor with a resounding thud. The bag which had been so light for the small and wheezy Henri, was clearly still extremely heavy for Banzai, despite his muscles.

"I think we'd better finish emptying it," said Horatio firmly, fixing Banzai with a look which meant business.

"Righty-O!" said Banzai, trying to lighten the atmosphere. He cautiously approached his bag once more and, with a sigh of resignation, he delved back inside it.

He scrabbled about inside the almost empty bag for a suspiciously long time. Eventually he emerged with a small earthenware jar. It wasn't very big but it seemed to be very heavy to Banzai, whose arms trembled slightly as he held it up for Horatio and Henri to see.

Chapter Four

The Cat's Out of the Bag

T he jar was small and plain. It was made of clay and had a tightly fitting lid which was fixed on with a ribbon and a wax seal. Banzai's eyes filled with tears (again) as he looked at the jar. He passed it to Horatio who was surprised by how light it was. He was even more surprised by how heavy it seemed to be for Banzai to hold.

"What's this?" he asked, as he took the jar from Banzai's trembling paws.

"G – Gu – Gran – Grandfather," gulped Banzai.

"Grandfather was also a ship's cat and he was the only one in the family who wasn't cross with me when I left school and ran away to sea. I last saw him when we both happened to be in Casablanca – I was travelling on a different ship at that time, before I joined The Beagle. He was very old even then (he estimated he must have been about 287 in cat years) and knew he wouldn't have many years left. He asked me to find the perfect place for his ashes to be buried when he had passed on to his next life.

"And that is the problem," continued Banzai. "He said that after spending all his life at sea, avoiding falling into it at all costs, he most certainly didn't want to be buried in the sea like lots of sailors. He wanted to have his ashes somewhere on dry land with a lovely view of the sea and where he would be very safe and very dry. I have been carrying Grandfather all over the world with me – being careful not to lose him or get him wet or covered in glitter – and I can't seem to find the right place to put his ashes."

Horatio felt very sorry for Banzai. His grandfather can't have known what a heavy burden this would turn out to be for one proud little cat who never liked to ask others for help.

Banzai was wailing a bit. "Poor Grandfather needs somewhere to rest – and I promised him! He spent all of his life travelling round and round the world – I'm sure he doesn't want to spend his AFTER life doing the same!"

Horatio walked over to his desk on which there stood a huge globe. He spun it gently round on its axis as Banzai wailed on.

"Poor Grandfather – he needs to be safely on dry land with a lovely view of the sea which he had loved to sail ON and look AT and fish FROM but did not want to be IN. During all his life and many years spent at sea he never fell in – he was a cat after all, and we hate water. And anyway, he couldn't swim."

Banzai prided himself on keeping promises. He might be a bit naughty and really quite fighty, but he always kept promises. He just couldn't find the perfect place for his rather fussy grandfather.

"What about somewhere in Sweden? There's an island off Stockholm which would be beautiful," suggested Horatio, peering at the globe.

"Too cold," said Banzai. "Grandfather always felt the cold – blue nose and stone cold paws most of the time and he once got frostbite on the tip of his tail, which meant he had to wear a bobble hat on it whenever he went anywhere even slightly cool."

Horatio spun the globe once again.

"What about Antigua? A beautiful island in the sun. My pirate aunt told me about a place there well away from the sea but with a beautiful view of it all around. From there you can see Nelson's Dockyard – I have the same first name as him you know?" Horatio was quite excited at the idea.

"Too hot," replied Banzai. "Grandfather hated getting sweaty. It made his fur clump together and gave him a headache. He usually had to lie in a hammock in the shade if he sailed to hot countries. The heat made him very irritable."

"What about Monastery Island?" exclaimed Horatio who was looking out of the window. "It's so close that you could just look up from St Benfro any time you choose and see where your grandfather is resting!" Horatio thought this idea was perfect – and Monastery Island would be easy to get to.

"Too close," said Banzai quickly. "Grandfather was proud to be a sailor and he thought that any land you could just about row to from St Benfro didn't really count as a voyage and he wanted his resting place to always involve a voyage."

"How about the Hebrides?" suggested Horatio.

"Not enough people," answered Banzai. "Grandfather always liked a bit of company."

"Somewhere in China?" said Horatio. "That is a long way from here – too far to row, but closer to Siam where he was born and that might be nice for him."

"Too many people," said Banzai bleakly. "Grandfather liked company but he didn't like crowds or to be disturbed if he was thinking or sleeping or just – just generally looking about."

Horatio wearily sat down in his wing-backed chair.

"I can see that this is your big problem Banzai. This is the big heavy one which has burdened you for so long. A promise not kept, guilt and a very fussy dead grandfather to make happy!" Horatio Fox wasn't often defeated by problems but this one was very tricky.

"Yes he was difficult to please," agreed Banzai. "That's why he spent his whole life at sea – always looking for the perfect place to live. And he never found it. Now the problem's mine and I'm stuck and poor Grandfather is still travelling the world – with me."

The room fell into silence until a little wheezy cough announced the presence of Henri. Horatio and Banzai had been so busy spinning the globe and squashing suggestions that they had forgotten the little pug was there. Evening had long-since closed in and the room was quite dark in the corners, making Henri difficult to see.

"What about Venice?" suggested Henri.

Horatio and Banzai looked at one another.

It was the perfect solution. Not too cold and not too hot. It would mean a voyage from St Benfro. There were lots of people so it was busy but it wasn't too crowded. In fact Grandfather had always loved sailing there because it was where merchants and traders from the East and the West could meet, exchange stories and do business. Banzai couldn't think of a single objection that Grandfather might have had. For the first time in many days Banzai breathed out – and smiled.

It was getting late and was already dark. Horatio suggested that Banzai should stay at Gunfort Mansions for the night, as he had a suggestion to help with the sheaf of letters. And little Henri, who had saved the day, trotted away home along the harbour wall – glittering as he went.

I wonder who he'd been cuddling, then?

When Henri had gone home, Horatio Fox made mugs of hot chocolate for himself and Banzai, and then he went to his glass artefacts cabinet and took out an ornate pair of spectacles. He handed them to Banzai who looked at him uncertainly.

"Thank you Horatio," he said. "I'm quite tired but I can still see you perfectly well." Banzai was puzzled.

"These are very particular and unusual spectacles," said Horatio. "You have a lot of letters to read and you might be glad of them."

"Yes but . . ." started Banzai.

"They are yours to keep and use for as long as you need them," said Horatio. "I'm going to bed now and I strongly recommend that you use these Reading Glasses when looking at your letters." And he left the room.

And for once, Banzai did as he was told.

He sat by the fireside with the sheaf of letters and put on the Reading Glasses. As he sat in the glow of a lamp, he found that by peering through the lenses of the Reading Glasses, the letters and words which had never made any sense to him before became clear to him. Magically and mysteriously, he could read! They were real READING glasses!

Two hours later he could hardly tear himself away to go to bed. He had read all his letters, which made him feel much better because his mama was not at all angry. She was just sending him news from home and hoping he was happy on board The Beagle and living in St Benfro. There had been no need to feel guilty and worried for all these years. If only he had faced up to the problem sooner he wouldn't have been weighed down with shame and needless worry.

When he had read the letters he had started to read Horatio's books. He found stories from ancient Greece about sailors who had fantastic adventures on a voyage called The Odyssey. He read poems about all kinds of beautiful places and interesting people including an owl and a pussy cat who went on a strange little voyage to a place where the Bong Tree grows. He could read anything he looked at including books written in Latin and a really wonderful book called Dr.Johnson's Dictionary, which didn't seem to have much of a story, but was full of beautiful words and interesting facts.

He was disturbed from his reading by a Spanish ship's clock on the mantelpiece striking eight bells. Midnight. (*Yes – ship's clocks are different*). Banzai picked up Mr.Wong and went to Horatio's spare room, where there was a huge feather bed waiting for him. He had only ever slept in baskets and hammocks before and he found himself purring as he hopped into the cloudy softness of bed, wearing his silk pyjamas and feeling very special indeed. The weight of his bag had finally been lifted from Banzai's tired little shoulders and now he could enjoy his dreams.

Yet in the darkness of the drawing room, the carpet bag was a lot lighter but not actually quite empty. There was something small and very shiny in a little dark pocket inside. A tiny golden brooch in the shape of a ship with a diamond at the top of the mast, which seemed to be easily forgotten.

Chapter Five

Banzai Vanishes

B anzai woke before dawn the next morning.
He hopped out of the lovely big feather bed
and immediately did his press-ups and expert
kickboxing moves. He hadn't slept for long but he had
slept deeply for the first time in years. He'd had no
nightmares about being chased or being alone on a raft
in the middle of the ocean or trapped in a dungeon with
no door. He knew he had important things to do and now
he felt strong enough to do them.

Still in his silk pyjamas, Banzai crept silently down the landing and past the room where Horatio could be heard softly snoring in his dream-filled sleep. He crept on through the drawing room and past the floppy carpet bag to the foot of a spiral staircase which led up to the turret above. He twirled round and round the flight of steps and up into the circular telescope room.

In the grey gloom of early morning, he could make out the outline of Horatio's huge Talking Telescope which was already looking out through a window towards the East and waiting for the sun to come up.

Even though Banzai knew this was Horatio's famous magical Talking Telescope, it still made him jump as he stepped out into the turret and heard it say, in a whispery hum, "Good morning Banzai – hmmmmm – I've been expecting you."

Banzai stammered good morning and asked if he could look through the huge lens towards the harbour. The telescope was happy to oblige and suggested that Banzai should open one of the windows to get a clear view of the sleepy ships far below.

The cold morning air rushed into the warmth of the room as if it had been waiting impatiently outside all night. Banzai didn't mind – he hardly even noticed. He climbed onto the footplate of the giant telescope and held on as it gently turned towards the open window and focused on The Beagle below.

"There's Grubson's Beagle," explained the telescope. "Hmmmm – Only Marjorie on board. Still sleeping. Hmmmm – Beagle almost seaworthy again. Just needs sails to be rigged and new helm to be adjusted," the telescope went on. Banzai was in shocked admiration of how much the telescope knew about everything it focused on – no wonder Horatio Fox seemed to know exactly what was going on in St Benfro.

"I need a ship to take me to London, St Malo, Seville and Venice. As soon as possible," whispered Banzai.

"Hmmmm, let me have a look . . ." the telescope gently moved its lens from The Beagle to another ship anchored nearby. Banzai peered eagerly through the viewing glass as the telescope moved from one ship to the next. The sun had just peeped up over the horizon and turned everything pink as the telescope said, "The Resolve. Hmmmm – Captain Dogmael's ship The Resolve is bound for Venice. He trades all over Europe. Hmmmm – Usual trading route for Captain Dogmael. Wool from St Benfro to be delivered to ports in England, France, Spain and Italy. Hmmmm – taking on board passengers in London, collecting brandy and lace from St Malo, oranges and leather boots in Seville and returning with silks from the Orient traded through Venice from where he will also bring back glassware from Murano. Hmmmm . . ."

Banzai was amazed not only at how much the Talking Telescope could see but also at his luck. Captain Dogmael was due to be sailing to all the cities Banzai needed to go!

"When does she sail?" asked Banzai in a stage whisper.

"Hmmmm – this morning, Banzai. The Resolve sails on the morning tide. Here comes Captain Dogmael now."

Banzai could see the shape of Captain Dogmael (a smart and efficient collie) hunched against the cold, walking towards his ship. Dogmael squinted as he looked up to the new sunrise and flipped open his pocket watch – he was obviously thinking about leaving harbour soon.

"Hmmmm – you need to be quick if you're going, Banzai. Good luck and fair weather!"

Banzai gabbled his thanks to the Talking Telescope, as he jumped down from the footplate and whisked down the spiral staircase.

Grabbing his empty carpet bag, he refilled it. In went his best bandana (he was wearing his everyday one), bulbs of fresh garlic, his brass telescope, the magical Reading Glasses, a copy of *Gulliver's Travels* (borrowed from Horatio's bookshelf), one money bag, Grandfather's jar and Mr.Wong. He carefully folded his silk pyjamas and left them tucked neatly under the pillow on the feather bed – he was hoping for another chance to sleep here when he returned. He left the sheaf of letters underneath a large ammonite fossil on Horatio's desk.

Then, using the back of one his mama's letters, he managed to write a note – well, scratch out some inky scrawlings – for Captain Grubson.

MY MOST DEEREST AND ~~ESTEAMED~~ ~~EXSTEEM~~ BEST FREND AND SKIPPER - GRUBSON!

IT IS WITH MY ~~ARROLO~~ ~~AROLL~~ SO SORRY BUT I MUST GO AWAY FOR A LITTLE WILE TO SORT OUT MY BAG WITCH HAS A ~~KURROL~~ ~~2 OR 3 4 OR 5~~ SUM PROBBLIMS AND IS CAWSING ME SUM TRUBBLE.

I DON'T NO HOW LONG I WILL BEE. BUT NOT TO LONG I HOPE. I EXPECK TO BE BACK BEFOUR THE BEAGLE IS FIXED. BEST YOU JUST THINK OF IT AS A LITTEL HOLLYDAY FOR BANZAI.

LIKE YOU SED - SURE LEVE.

BACK SOON. DON'T WURRY.

CHIN UP!

TOODLE-OO

BANZAI!

Lifting his bag over his shoulder once more, he quietly let himself out of Horatio's flat and hurried down the eight flights of stairs. From the turret, Horatio's Talking Telescope watched as Banzai slipped about on the snowy pavement below and carefully picked his way around the harbour wall and onto The Beagle. Banzai pushed the crinkly letter in its reused envelope through the door of the wheelhouse and left the ship without making a sound. The telescope grinned as it watched him stand on the gangway for The Resolve and speak to Captain Dogmael. Banzai was doing some fast talking and showing off his muscles. After some minutes he produced some gold coins from his carpet bag. Captain Dogmael smiled broadly at the little cat and welcomed him on board The Resolve.

"Hmmmm…"

The wind was blowing strongly as the tide changed direction and Captain Dogmael gave the order to weigh anchor. The Resolve slipped quietly out of harbour and away towards the horizon, bound for London.

If Banzai had looked back to St Benfro, he might have seen a tiny figure sitting on the harbour wall watching The Resolve sail away. Henri patiently watched her leaving, shivering in the cold but warmed with dreams of being a sailor one day. Little did he know who was on board with Captain Dogmael.

When The Resolve was nothing more than a black speck of sail on the horizon, Henri continued on his way to Gunfort Mansions. The postman had brought another letter for Banzai that morning and Henri wanted to take it to him as soon as he could. He recognised the stamp and the writing but this time it also had the words URGENT and IMPORTANT written on the back of the envelope in bright red ink.

Up in the turret of Gunfort Mansions, Horatio had seen Henri on the harbour wall. He too had seen The Resolve leave port. Watching through his Talking Telescope, he had seen Banzai on board and listened as his telescope filled him in on all the details.

"Hmmmm – Banzai on board The Resolve sailing to London, St Malo, Seville and Venice."

Horatio understood why Banzai had gone, but he wasn't sure how Grubson or anyone else would feel about his sudden disappearance. A very impetuous cat, that Banzai. His thoughts had been interrupted by the telescope changing its focus to Henri trotting along towards the flat.

"Henri on his way," said the telescope. "Hmmmm – bringing an URGENT and IMPORTANT letter for Banzai. Hmmmm . . . Too late."

Horatio was waiting with his front door open as his little friend wheezed up the eight flights of stairs and arrived on his doorstep waving a letter for Banzai.

Chapter Six

URGENT and IMPORTANT

Henri's face fell as Horatio explained that Banzai had gone. If he was going all the way to Venice on board The Resolve with Captain Dogmael it would be many weeks before he returned. What about the URGENT and IMPORTANT letter?

Opening someone else's letter is a very serious business and both Horatio and Henri were hesitant about doing this. It was propped up against the Spanish ship's clock on the mantelpiece and seemed to be attracting stray flakes of glitter which were still drifting in the air from Mr.Wong's silvery threads. The minutes ticked by, the letter seemed to sparkle in the morning light and the red inked URGENT and IMPORTANT shone more brightly.

"Henri, I would never usually do this," started Horatio as he picked up his ivory letter-opener. "But Banzai has trusted us with the contents of his carpet bag and he has shared his deepest secrets with us. I don't think he would mind if we open his letter."

"And it does say URGENT and IMPORTANT," agreed Henri.

"And we don't know exactly when he will be back from Venice with Captain Dogmael," added Horatio.

He sliced open the flimsy envelope and extracted the tissue-paper letter.

My dear Banzai
I hope you find someone to help you read this letter (you silly lad for not staying at school).
It is URGENT and IMPORTANT.
Your sister Katinka's smallest son Bonsai has run away to sea! He took his knitten, a bandana and a chicken sandwich. He left a very badly written note to say he has gone to Europe to find you because you are his hero and he wants to meet you and sail around the world with you.
He is very young – only three and although he thinks he's tough, he's only a kitten.
Please find him – you'll know him when you see him.
Love from your worried Mama XXX

Henri was trembling as he listened to the words of the letter. Poor little Bonsai – alone in the world – at sea. What could he do? Who could help?

"Papa!" shouted Henri.

With that, Horatio and Henri pulled on their hats and scarves and ran down to the street below and along the harbour wall towards The Beagle. They hadn't even made it to the end of the wall before they saw Grubson Pug stomping along through the snow from his ship. He was still growling under his breath as he re-read Banzai's crinkly note. Grubson was surprised to see his youngest son and Horatio Fox running towards him waving another tissue-paper letter.

Not long afterwards there was a lot of activity on board The Beagle. The shipwrights were instructed to hurry to make everything shipshape and ready for a voyage. They set to work attaching sails to the rigging and adjusting the new helm, whilst Grubson went ashore to order supplies of fresh water, food and rum. Then he rushed to the exchange to let the wool merchants know that he would be sailing in the morning and to deliver their fleeces to The Beagle without delay.

Marjorie, who usually preferred to travel everywhere by ship or by carriage, was ready for action too. She preened her feathers and did a few chest expanding exercises before flying West to Barafundle Bay to tell Sebastian to come back to The Beagle. She then headed North East to Carew Castle to deliver the same message to Lefty. The two dogs headed back to St Benfro by road whilst Marjorie flew all the way home, very pleased with herself and resolving to do more flying even though she was a very old parrot.

Grubson was pleased to be going back to sea, even if it was a last-minute rush. During one of his quieter moments, he saw Horatio and Henri standing together huddled against the cold, watching all the frantic activity. Grubson knew what Henri wanted more than anything and he knew that Horatio's ancestor had been a famous seafarer – a pirate no less. Without them, he wouldn't know where Banzai was and he wouldn't be going on this voyage.

Hurrying up the gangplank he called over to the two friends.

"Henri – go and get my charts and tide-tables from my study please – they'll be needed on the voyage. Then perhaps both of you would like to pack a few things in a bag and meet me here on board The Beagle at supper time. You're coming too!"

URGENT and IMPORTANT

The next morning, Horatio's Talking Telescope watched as The Beagle weighed anchor at first light and slipped away from St Benfro. Down on the harbour wall, Adele Grubson and three of her children waved them off. Her fourth child was on board ship waving back to his family and St Benfro for the first time in his life. He was thrilled to be accompanying Grubson on board The Beagle. His friend Horatio was just as excited and hoped his pirate aunt wouldn't mind that he was wearing her big thick coat to keep him warm on the voyage.

Lefty and Sebastian were busy with ropes and sails as The Beagle left the calm of the harbour behind and struck out into deeper waters. The wind filled her new sails and Grubson was smiling happily as he stood at the shiny new helm and guided his beloved ship out on the first voyage of the new year.

The only thing missing from The Beagle, that made each member of the crew feel a bit sad, was Banzai. They were used to having the cheeky ship's cat sitting way up high in his crow's nest, eye to his telescope, scanning the horizon and watching out for rocks and pirates. They even missed the whiff of garlic on the air. But Banzai was the whole reason for this urgent and important voyage and they set to work even harder to help The Beagle pick up speed and chase The Resolve on her voyage across Europe to Venice

Chapter Seven

London

Four days after leaving St Benfro, The Resolve sailed up the Thames in the dawn light. London loomed out of the thick morning fog ballooning up from the deep cold river. Captain Dogmael's cat, Tom, was up in the crow's nest doing his best to look out for the huge barges, big galleons and tiny rowing boats which were hidden within the grey folds of fog. But it was impossible. The only way to avoid collisions was by listening. Low, booming bass notes of foghorns signalled the presence of barges, urgent bells rang out at regular intervals from galleons and the rowers either tooted small hooters or shouted into the fog. Even this early in the morning, the Thames was noisy with an eerie orchestra of sound from the invisible vessels.

Whilst Tom rang a brass bell from the nest, Banzai scooted around the deck helping out where he could, calling into the fog to warn other river users that The Resolve was coming through – even though it wasn't strictly his job and he could have just stayed in his hammock drinking tea and snoozing. But sailing gets into your blood and it was his instinct to keep the ship safe.

When The Resolve was safely moored at Tower Bridge, Captain Dogmael set off into the City to buy and sell his goods, leaving instructions that the crew and ship were to be ready to set sail again on the evening tide. He liked to be early to the markets where he could set his prices without too much competition. Having sold his cargo he would then meet old friends in The Dog and Compass behind St Paul's Cathedral. The cold glass of the windows was fugged with hot breath and as Dogmael entered the pub, the smell of steamy damp fur forced him to pant shallow breaths as he closed the door behind him. This was where he could count on meeting his fellow captains and merchants. This was where he could agree some nice low prices to buy more cargo before sailing on across Europe. Captain Dogmael was a very busy captain and he wasted no time.

Banzai picked up his carpet bag and set off into town. He also knew exactly what he was doing and where he was going, but he told no one. The Resolve's crew assumed he was off to arm-wrestle in bars – he was famous for it and each of them had been caught out by him in the past. But he hurried straight past all the riverside bars and whisked down a narrow cobbled alley between buildings. The fog thickened into the space where Banzai had been only moments earlier and he had once more, performed a vanishing act. When he returned to The Resolve a few hours later, Banzai stayed very quiet about where he had been and disappeared to his cabin where he spent the rest of the day with his nose in a book – reading!

Who would have thought it? Banzai the reader – now that he had the magical Reading Glasses, he could hardly stop doing it and he was really enjoying the strange and mysterious travels of someone called Gulliver.

That afternoon brought a lot of activity around The Resolve as passengers boarded for their journey to Venice and various goods were delivered in crates to be taken on to France and beyond. No one particularly noticed the Siamese cat who kept himself to himself and seemed to be a bit of a bookworm. However everyone definitely noticed the niff of garlic which seemed to permeate throughout the ship, yet no one could work out where it came from.

Banzai felt a bit odd being on board a ship as a passenger. He was used to having plenty of jobs to do and he missed being up in the crow's nest. The Resolve's cat was a very old moggy called Tom. He and Dogmael had travelled all around the world together over many years. Tom was a good sailor but his weary old bones and creaky limbs were a problem to him. Banzai noticed that it took him a good half hour to climb up the rigging and the masts to the crow's nest – and he was pretty sure that Tom was snoozing too much of the time, when he should have been on look-out duty.

That evening, preparing to leave London, it was painful to see the scrawny old cat hoist his rickety frame from rope to rope. Dogmael held his breath as his moth-eaten cat struggled  higher up the mast and Banzai could hardly bear to watch the

slow grinding climb. Muttering to himself as he went, Tom hauled himself up the rigging and wobbled out along the yardarm before he finally tipped himself head first into the crow's nest. After a couple of minutes of scrabbling and puffing noises, Tom's old grey head appeared over the side and having adjusted his eye-patch, he gave Dogmael the thumbs up.

"Off we go then," said Captain Dogmael quietly under his breath. Then he raised his voice, shouted his orders to the rest of the crew, the anchor was weighed and off they went – leaving London in the sunset, bound for France.

The following morning, The Beagle came into London's port and moored up.

Grubson made a few enquiries and discovered that The Resolve had been and gone already – bound for St Malo. He had half-expected this because Captain Dogmael was well-known for always being in a hurry. When he had completed his merchant business for the day, Grubson settled down with Henri in the wheel-house where they carefully examined the tide-tables and charts to plan the next stage of their voyage to St Malo in France.

Henri was feeling sick with excitement at the prospect of crossing the Channel for the first time in his life.

Horatio was feeling sick with the rocking motion of the ship, which upset his balance and made him feel a bit queasy.

Lefty and Sebastian had suggested all kinds of remedies for seasickness, including looking at the horizon, not looking at the horizon, drinking large quantities of rum and singing sea shanties to take his mind off it. None of these suggestions had worked and he was resigned to feeling a bit off-colour for a few days until he got used to it.

Grubson and his crew usually liked to stay in each city for a day or two but this voyage was different – they were desperate to catch up with The Resolve and Banzai. So that evening The Beagle slid out of London and hurried off towards France. This was a route the crew knew well and they worked as a team pulling on ropes, hoisting sails and trying to catch the best wind. Marjorie now had two jobs on board The Beagle as she flew between the galley where she made food for the hungry crew and the crow's nest where she kept an eye out for rocks and pirates. Henri was staring at the sea charts, trying to see the quickest way to St Malo to make up some time. But The Beagle was still a whole day and night behind The Resolve and everyone knew that Captain Dogmael liked to sail fast. The chase was on.

Chapter Eight

St Malo

After eight days and nights of hard sailing across the Channel, The Resolve arrived in St Malo just before midnight. The medieval buttresses of the town looked like huge castle ramparts in the darkness and there was not much sign of life from the outside. Inside the town, most of the inhabitants were asleep. The waves thrashed against the ancient sea walls and sent seaweed ribboning across the roads in the town. Aboard The Resolve, the crew and all the passengers lay asleep in their beds, waiting for the sun to rise.

In the morning, Captain Dogmael and Banzai strolled into town together. Dogmael was off to the market to sell fleeces and buy brandy and lace for shopkeepers back in St Benfro. He liked Banzai and was inquisitive about why he was travelling as a passenger on The Resolve, when everyone knew he was the ship's cat for The Beagle. Dogmael asked Banzai what plans he had for the day. But the secretive cat simply shrugged his shoulders in a very French way and said he had no special plans but would just wander for a while and have a little poke about and possibly buy some lovely French garlic. He shrugged again.

As Dogmael and Banzai parted ways, the Captain shouted a reminder to him that they would be leaving on the evening tide and not to be late back to the harbour. He looked back over his shoulder to see whether Banzai had heard him and just glimpsed the bright red polka dot bandana on Banzai's head, as he purposefully threaded his way through the crowds of shoppers and sailors, hurrying away down a narrow cobbled street. Captain Dogmael didn't think Banzai looked as if he was just having an aimless wander. Where was he going?

By the time Captain Dogmael had completed his business with the merchants of St Malo, Banzai was already back on board The Resolve with the rest of the passengers. The crew had restocked and loaded new cargo into the hold. Captain Dogmael ran a very tight ship and they were all ready to leave as soon as the evening tide was up.

Everyone on board The Resolve was leaning over the port side of the ship to watch the beautiful sight of St Malo in the golden rays of a sinking sun.

Had they happened to glance over to starboard, they would have seen The Beagle rolling into view at full sail, hurrying to reach St Malo before the evening turned to night.

Meanwhile everyone on board The Beagle was very busy controlling the ship as she headed fast into St Malo – a tricky harbour at the best of times due to all the islands and rocks at the entrance to the port. They didn't have time to notice The Resolve heading in the opposite direction.

They were very much like two ships that pass in the night.

Grubson nodded in a resigned kind of way when the French harbourmaster explained that The Resolve had been and gone in a very quick turnaround.

"That Dogmael," said the Frenchman. "He in a beeg fat hurry to get to Seville, non? Always he's with the beeg fat hurry," he muttered shaking his head disapprovingly.

The Beagle and her crew moored up in the space which had just been vacated by The Resolve.

"We might not be catching up with Captain Dogmael, but at least we're no further behind," pointed out Horatio.

"That's true," agreed Grubson. "But although I want my Banzai back on board as soon as we catch up with them, I never hurry away from St Malo. It's the home of my ancestors and I have a lot of relatives here."

Captain Grubson and the entire crew left the ship and spent the day with his relatives: Les Grubsons, as the French end of the family was known.

Cousin Guillaume ran a restaurant in a very unusual building. Like Grubson's house in St Benfro, it had a wonderful view of the sea and was a landmark for the town. Unlike Grubson's house which was on top of the harbour wall at St Benfro, Guillaume's restaurant was part of the harbour wall. It stood proud of the wall by three storeys and the front door was just inside a porch within the wall itself. The town side of the building was brightly lit in the evenings with candles shining from every window and was a welcome sight for tired merchants and hungry sea dogs needing a good meal. From the sea side of the building it was a different story. The sea pounded the restaurant with every breath it took – waves unfurling against the walls and huge reinforced windows. On stormy days or full moon nights, when the tide and the waves were swollen and angry, the brave little building withstood a bashing.

Guillaume wasn't afraid. He made the windows which looked out to sea as big as possible and on stormy days, the diners sitting closest to those windows were treated to an underwater view of everything beneath the waves. Henri was nervous as he first approached the table which had been reserved for the extended Grubson gathering. Padded seats were patted for him to come and sit close to aunts and cousins and he obediently jumped up next to a kindly old lady called Great Aunt Celeste.

Great Aunt Celeste cuddled Henri close to her pearl-laden chest as he cowered away from the large Sea Window – uncertain about the seaweed, shells and pebbles which regularly battered against the glass. He was even more uncertain as he saw surprised lobsters suddenly flatten against the window with an enforced view of the restaurant within. Had they had time before being dragged back seawards again by the current, they would have seen some of their own relatives, looking equally surprised, staring out from a glass tank inside the restaurant – waiting to be chosen as someone's main course.

"Alors! La bas – cette langoustine avec les grandes yeux! "

"There – that lobster with the big eyes!" translated Great Aunt Celeste for the confused pup. Henri tried not to look at the lobsters inside the tank but he couldn't help looking up every time he heard the clack of shell against glass and another startled lobster whisked past the huge Sea Window.

Guillaume looked very like his cousin Grubson – with just the addition of a very carefully waxed and curled moustache. He loved to entertain in his restaurant and proudly twisted his whiskers into a finer curl as he glanced around the huge table where seventeen Grubson family members were enjoying his fabulous food. "Zis is most fine, non?" he said. "Mon famille – we are all gazzered 'ere Chez Guillaume, where we eat ze finest lobster and fruits of the sea. Where we can tell ze stories of ze sailing and beeg voyages. I am very contented – très content. And now – as you say – tuck in!"

After a big seafood stew, laced with garlic (which just made the crew miss Banzai even more), Les Grubsons listened to the story of the shipwreck off Monastery Island open-mouthed. They were horrified at the dangerous winter storm and enthralled to hear how The Beagle had been saved by the Christmas presents. They commiserated with Grubson about his missing cat and, to distract them all from tales of unreliable cats and bad luck at sea, they lifted their spirits with French sea songs accompanied by Guillaume's youngest son Jacques, on his accordion.

Little Henri spent most of the evening being passed between uncles and aunts who all thought he was "Très gentil" and wanted to cuddle him and kiss him on both cheeks. His face was aching from the pressing of pursed lips and slightly pink from Great Aunt Celeste's Rose Allure lipstick. His tummy was full of beautiful food and flavours of herbs and he was starting to get the hang of French as le petit Jacques taught him French songs.

He felt very happy "très content" to be in France with his French family and was reluctant to leave Chez

Guillaume until he remembered Bonsai – lost somewhere in Europe. Grubson glanced out of the Sea Window and declared that the tide was turning and they would soon need to set sail if they were to catch up with The Resolve and help Banzai's little nephew.

An hour later, The Beagle was waved off by Les Grubsons who stood on top of the harbour wall like a string of happy onions – waving as she sailed out in pursuit of The Resolve. "Bon voyage," called Grubson's cousins as they waved him goodbye, "et bonne chance pour la chasse!"

Chapter Nine

Seville

After four days of very lumpy seas in the Bay of Biscay, followed by five days of fair weather and full sails down the coast of Portugal, The Resolve came to a stop in the harbour of Seville. The final port before heading straight for Venice.

They arrived on the midday tide and everyone on board felt better in the warmer winds and winter sunshine. Tom stayed up in the crow's nest, exhausted after the last leg of the voyage. He was on his last legs himself and decided to have a snooze in his eyrie, whilst everyone else got to work off-loading cargo and taking wool to the market.

Amidst all the activity on deck, Dogmael noticed Banzai go ashore with the carpet bag which never left his side. He waved goodbye but the little cat, who had spent most of the voyage reading in his cabin, seemed to have his mind on other things as he trotted down the gangplank and away into the town. Very purposefully.

The passengers and crew from The Resolve made the most of being back on land and enjoyed the lively atmosphere in Seville.

Once more, Captain Dogmael went to the market with fleeces. Even in the winter, Seville felt warm – the wind, although cold, didn't have the bite of more northern countries. Wrapped in big coats and wearing broad-rimmed felt hats, the customers of bars and cafes stubbornly sat outside at pavement tables to catch any winter warmth. Street traders passed between tables showing trinkets and jewellery, jugglers demonstrated their skills, upturned hats at their feet waiting for payment. Dogmael paused briefly to watch the activities and even stayed long enough to dance with a particularly pretty senorita whose dark eyes and long lashes caused him to briefly forget why he was there. After a little tango and a flourish of a borrowed tambourine, Dogmael bowed very low to the alluring lady before he reluctantly turned away and headed to the wool market.

Towards the end of the day, Captain Dogmael was returning to the harbour (keeping an eye out for the lovely senorita whose perfume still lingered on his jacket) when he was surprised to see Tom. He had thought that Tom would still be snoring up in the crow's nest, but he appeared to have got some energy back as he stood beneath the empty orange trees in the market square, talking to a very ancient and exotic cat sporting a knee-length long grey beard. They were both laughing like children as they pulled on the strings of two beautiful multi-coloured kites which danced in the brisk breezes above them. Tom's kite was bobbing and diving, twirling its tail ribbons and skimming the tree tops as he deftly tweaked and rolled the strings. Intrigued by his old cat, Dogmael was unseen by Tom as he successfully seemed to haggle with the bearded cat. After quite some time, the two cats smiled at one another and clasped paws. A deal had been made which involved Tom proudly handing over a box of bright hand-made kites as he carefully accepted a nice fat purse of coins from the kite trader. "Cats", thought Dogmael, "Just when you think you've got to know them and they're still full of surprises."

Back at the harbour-side, crates of oranges and boxes of leather boots were delivered to the ship ready to sell in Venice. It was a busy time and, as usual, Captain Dogmael was in a hurry to complete his business and head off to Venice. That was the main aim of this voyage and he was looking forward to getting to Italy where he had a special old friend to see. By noon the following day The Resolve was loaded and ready to go. Banzai had completed his business too and he was trying not to watch as yet again Tom started his long climb up to the crow's nest. Banzai thought he should offer to help, but he didn't want to offend the old ship's cat. After all, he wouldn't like it if another cat took his job on board The Beagle!

Captain Dogmael knew that Tom would need to retire soon, but he didn't want to offend his old friend and was waiting for the right time to suggest this to him. Dogmael liked to do everything double-quick at top speed and Tom had become so terribly old and slow. He really should stay ashore in St Benfro and put his feet up by the fireside on these cold winter days. Poor Tom – he would find it hard to become a landlubber and stop his ocean-going life, and Dogmael just couldn't find the right words to ask him to retire.

Poor Tom – he was desperately trying to find a way to explain to Captain Dogmael that he was too old for all this sailing malarkey. He found the heavy winter seas too rough for his old bones now and he didn't think his eyesight (in his one good eye) was as sharp as it should be for a look-out. And to be honest, he couldn't help falling asleep when he knew he should be keeping watch. But Dogmael would surely be so upset to lose his favourite old sailing friend. How could he find a way to explain to Dogmael that he wanted to retire? He wanted to stay home in St Benfro with his feet up by the fire in the winter and he dreamed of selling kites on the beach in the summer. Poor Dogmael

– how would he find a replacement cat for the good ship Resolve?

With Tom finally installed in the crow's nest once more, Captain Dogmael gave the order and The Resolve moved out of harbour. The crew was very busy as they carefully manoeuvred past all the other ships and smaller boats which were crammed in the busy harbour. Then they had to navigate their way down the river and out to the open sea beyond.

So no one took any notice as they passed The Beagle on her way up the river towards Seville.

But on board The Beagle, Henri and Horatio had been the first to spot The Resolve and they jumped around on deck waving their arms, calling and shouting to her. Grubson was busy steering and Sebastian had his hands full furling in the sails, but Lefty also started to wave joined by a lot of squawking from Marjorie. The Beagle was very noisy indeed. But Tom was already asleep in his crow's nest and the rest of the crew on The Resolve were still fully occupied steering a great big ship down quite a narrow river.

However, The Resolve's passengers saw all the activity on board The Beagle and waved back to her, thinking she was a very friendly ship. Banzai was below deck in his cabin checking the contents of his bag and making sure everything was safe. As he took his head out of his bag and was picking some glitter off his fur, he thought he could hear a lot of shouting. He thought he might recognise some of the voices – especially a high pitched parrot? And was someone calling his name? It couldn't be though? The Beagle hadn't been ready to sail when he was last in St Benfro. It couldn't be Captain Grubson and the crew – could it?

By the time he got up on deck, the ships had passed and The Resolve was picking up speed towards the mouth of the river and the wide open sea. Looking back, Banzai could make out the familiar silhouette of The Beagle. His heart leapt – his friends – his ship! There was no point in shouting – The Resolve was sailing in the opposite direction fast. He suddenly missed his friends. Puzzled, and feeling quite homesick, he returned to his cabin and cuddled Mr.Wong who was always very comforting.

Meanwhile on board The Beagle, Henri was beside himself. So near – and yet so far.

"Don't worry son," said Grubson kindly. "We know The Resolve is off to Venice and we're only half a day behind them if we make haste in Seville and leave on the early tide."

Henri nodded. He knew his Papa was right, but he missed Banzai and he couldn't help worrying about the three year old Bonsai who was somewhere in Europe, looking for his uncle with only his knitten for a friend.

Chapter Ten

Death in Venice

During the seventeen days it had taken to sail across the Mediterranean and all the way down the coast of Italy and back up the other side to Venice, Captain Dogmael and Banzai had become firm friends.

It started off because poor old Tom was just too tired to keep climbing up and down to the crow's nest. On the third morning, he couldn't even get out of his hammock, never mind make the long climb. Captain Dogmael was very relieved when Banzai offered to help and, to everyone's

surprise, so was Tom. He grasped Banzai's shoulders and looked into his blue eyes (with his one good eye) as he thanked him for his help and then immediately fell into a deep and snoring sleep.

On the 16th of February, over a month since leaving St Benfro, The Resolve arrived in Venice on the morning tide. Banzai had a magnificent view of the graceful buildings from up in the crow's nest. It took his breath away. The watery city was just as Dogmael had described. Huge churches and palaces seemed to rise out of the water to cluster around the narrow canals and tiny alleyways. Winter sunlight glittered through the canals and bounced beneath the bridges, making everything glimmer and shimmy. Venice twinkled like a magical city in a dream where everything seemed to be made of light or water. But it was real and made of brick and stone. Although it might sound impossible, this beautiful and magnificent city was built on thousands and thousands of wooden stilts sunk deep into the water. Banzai stopped whistling and stared in wonder.

When The Resolve had moored, Banzai looked down from his vantage point and tried to make out where the sound of singing was coming from. He could see long, narrow, highly-polished black boats being propelled across the watery canals by water-rats using very long poles. They were the famous gondoliers who transferred the Venetian citizens around the waterways. Banzai could hear the gondoliers calling to one another and singing beautiful warbling songs as they skilfully guided their long gondolas up and down the narrow canals.

Banzai had enjoyed being back in a crow's nest with his telescope. He loved sailing and he liked being busy. Captain Dogmael had enjoyed having a ship's cat who could climb fast and see a long way. Dogmael was grateful for Banzai's help and asked him whether there was anything he could do to return the favour. After a bit of shrugging and garlic chewing Banzai decided to explain about needing to bury Grandfather's ashes in Venice. He asked Dogmael if he knew of just the perfect spot for Grandfather's final resting place.

Captain Dogmael smiled. He had a lot of friends in Venice and knew just the right water-rat to help them out.

A water-rat named Nautilus. He was the son of a son of a son of a son of a son of a gondolier. And all of his sons were gondoliers too. As were his nephews and cousins, uncles and brothers. In fact all the gondoliers were related. It was a family business.

The gondoliers were lively and cheeky and full of fun. They sang romantic ballads to lovers, funny ditties to those who seemed a bit gloomy and opera songs to anyone who would listen. Venice would not be Venice without Nautilus and his huge family of smiling, singing gondoliers.

Nautilus, with his long nose, twitchy whiskers, bright eyes, loud singing voice and jaunty hat was well known and liked throughout Venice. And he mostly liked to have fun. Which is why he loved children so much – they laugh and dance and sing at the slightest excuse and these were his favourite things to do too. Nautilus liked children so much that he and his wife had lots of them; their home was always cooing with babies in cots, always noisy with youngsters learning to talk, walk and swim. His family was so big that Nautilus was not always sure if there was anyone missing from the dinner table in the evening.

Dogmael knew that Nautilus would help and they set off to find him in his favourite bar near the Rialto Bridge.

Nautilus listened intently whilst Dogmael explained about the terrible problems that Banzai had been having with his Grandfather's ashes. He very much wanted to help this cat with his huge burden. He knew he could help but before he did anything else, Nautilus dried his eyes (he always cried when he heard sad stories) and gave the surprised Banzai a huge and very squeezy hug. Then he clasped his spindly paws together, smiled broadly and said that he knew just exactly the most perfect place for Grandfather.

There is an island in the Venice lagoon where all the Venetians are buried. It is called San Michele. It is a very peaceful place but not too far from the bustle and business of the city. There is a wall to keep it safe from flooding and the sea glitters all around. Banzai knew that Grandfather would be very happy to have his ashes buried here.

Nautilus was keen to get on with funeral arrangements straight away. He wanted to give Banzai's Grandfather the best send-off Venice could muster. A funeral to remember! He promised to return to The Resolve as soon as the sun had set and darkness had settled across the lagoon.

"Theese is the best I theenk, no?" said Nautilus. "Een-a the night time, with a beautiful shining moon in the sky for us to wish farewell to the Grandpapa of Banzai, no?"

Banzai nodded, wondering whether this idea was a little bit spooky but Nautilus seemed to know exactly what he was talking about and was clearly very enthusiastic about a night-time funeral. Nautilus gave him another big squeezy hug before jumping onto his gondola and hurrying away to find some of his relatives who would be needed for the funeral.

The market in Venice was a very loud and busy place. Merchants from China, Siam, Russia and Japan arrived in their unusual ships from the East. They traded loudly and with a lot of shouting and arm-waving with the merchants of Venice, France, Spain and from all over Europe including St Benfro far away to the West. Shouting and arm-waving seemed to be a good way for everyone to make themselves understood despite all the different languages.

The city went quieter as the sun set and everyone disappeared to their homes and ships for the night. Everyone apart from Nautilus and six of his brothers and nephews. They quietly steered their gondolas down the chilly waters of the Grand Canal and under the Rialto Bridge before stopping alongside The Resolve.

Banzai got onto Nautilus's gondola, which had been decorated with tiny red ribbons. Closely clutching the jar containing Grandfather's ashes, he stared up to the sky which was lit by the beautiful crescent moon. Dogmael and Tom got onto another gondola and the remaining five gondolas carried the rest of the crew and some of the passengers who wanted to pay their respects to the old sea cat. Huddled within blankets provided by the gondoliers, the funeral party was a little subdued by the freezing air, and the slightly chilling notion of what might happen in the cold darkness of San Michele.

When everyone was safely aboard, Nautilus and the gondoliers smoothly took them across the dark lagoon and out to the island of San Michele. Each passenger was given a lantern on the end of a long stick to light their way. The candles inside the lanterns jumped and flickered in the chilly night breeze and Banzai was filled with a sense of magic as the candle-light fleckled against the highly polished black boats. The gondoliers sung beautiful sad songs in voices that warbled and quivered up into the night sky and disappeared out to the frosty February stars beyond.

Out on the island, Nautilus led the way through the graveyard, followed by a string of dark figures, each carrying a candle-lantern. The tiny lights glowed against huge white tombstones which loomed out of the darkness and cast jumping shadows on the graves. The cold night breeze whispered through the leafless trees which made spooky silhouettes against the moonlight Banzai clutched Grandfather a little tighter to him, unsure if this was in fact the right place. But Nautilus jauntily walked on, encouraging the nervous funeral party with his gentle humming.

"'Ere it ees!" pronounced Nautilus loudly, breaking the silence. Banzai jumped at the sudden sound, but he just managed to avoid dropping Grandfather's jar.

In the candlelight, everyone could see a perfectly round mimosa tree at the edge of the graveyard. It was small enough not to draw attention to itself, yet big enough to give shade in the summer heat and shelter in the winter winds. It was near everyone else, but not too crowded. Best of all it had a beautiful view of the sea, but there was absolutely no chance of getting wet. Banzai knew that Nautilus had understood about Grandfather perfectly and had picked exactly the right resting place for him.

Grandfather's jar was tucked safely within the roots of the mimosa tree and covered with earth whilst the gondoliers sang a melancholy song of farewell. And then, because they all loved the sea and Grandfather had been a sailor all of his life, Banzai, Dogmael, Nautilus, the gondoliers, The Resolve's crew and passengers and even old creaky Tom, sang sea shanties and danced hornpipes under the moonlight.

Banzai didn't feel sad. How could he? He remembered that Grandfather had loved his life as a sailor and he had laughed a lot. As Nautilus said, anyone who has laughed a lot in their lifetime must be having a good time in the next life with the angels who like nothing more than to have a good laugh.

"Whaddya theenk 'eaven is a place full of angels cryin'? No my furry signor – eet is a full of angels laughin' and-a singin'. They ees 'appy to be in 'eaven, no? Eet is only us down 'ere that does sometimes the cryin'. But we can't stay cryin' for long. No signor. If we spend-a too long with the cryin' all the world, eet turn-a blurry and we can't see where we is goin'! Sometimes we grown-ups forget to laugh so much – but leesten to children, eh? They laugh all day if they is allowed to! They is like the angels – 'appy

and laughin' and take nothin' too serious. Let's live like angels, signor Banzai!"

The Beagle was arriving into Venice just as the little funeral flotilla was singing its candle-lit way back from the island of San Michele. Everyone on board saw the tiny lanterns shimmering against the dark waters of the lagoon and heard small but beautiful voices singing out across the water. As they watched and listened, the songs seemed to move to faster rhythms and brighter, cheekier tunes. Those were certainly sea shanties they could hear.

Through the darkness, Grubson was astonished to see the shape of a white cat sitting in one of the gondolas. The flickering candle revealed the familiar shape of a white cat with a bandana round his head! A familiar white cat singing at the top of his voice, as if he hadn't a care in the world.

Grubson smiled – he was relieved and happy to have found his favourite cat.

Banzai was relieved too – Grandfather was safe and happy with the angels on San Michele.

Chapter Eleven

San Marco

The following morning, as Venetians slept in their beds and sailors slept in their hammocks, a few gondoliers came out onto the water to prepare for a busy day ahead. There was something different in the air this morning – there was a distinct spark of excitement and expectation, as if the whole city was holding its breath, waiting to start something.

Woken by the clanging of hundreds of church bells, the crews aboard The Beagle and The Resolve leapt from their hammocks and shouted their "Hallos" to one another. Banzai and Dogmael were very surprised to see Grubson and his crew; they had no idea that The Beagle had been chasing them around Europe. Amongst all the sailor chat about their voyages and news from St Benfro, Henri and Horatio gave Banzai the latest letter from his mama. He quietly read it for himself and, without bothering to remove the Reading Glasses, he put his head back and wailed. Poor Banzai looked as if he had all the cares in the world on his shoulders again. He had just buried Grandfather and now his tiny nephew Bonsai was missing somewhere in Europe. How would they find him?

Captain Dogmael thought that Venice would be a very good place to start looking for the kitten. After all, this was the crossroads for East and West – it was very likely that the ship Bonsai had sailed on from Siam would have come to Venice.

A voice shouted up to them from the water below. Looking down, they could see Nautilus with some very strange looking passengers in his gondola. A lady dog was wearing a huge silk gown and a feathery mask over her face. Her friend was wearing a monk's hood but wore a mask like a bird. Their faces were almost hidden which made them rather unnerving.

"Carnevale!" exclaimed Nautilus. "Today everyone – they ees dressing up like-a strange weirdo characters eh? Like fine laydees and fine gentlemens – and sometimes like-a the bird creatures. Eet is huge fun to run around-a Venice in disguise being naughty, no? And-a nobody cares! Come and join in – we find you costumes! Today is for the meeschief!"

The two strange passengers got off the gondola and disappeared down a narrow alleyway, shrieking with excitement as they went. Dogmael quickly explained that they couldn't join in with Carnival because of the missing kitten. Nautilus went very quiet. His eyes filled (again) as he thought about little Bonsai – lost and alone.

A plan was hatched for everyone to split up and look for Bonsai – they would all recognise him when they saw him because he was a miniature version of Banzai. *And there are not too many of those around.*

Now there were three search parties.

Dogmael, Tom and the crew of The Resolve; Nautilus who told every gondolier he met as he punted his way around the maze of canals, and Grubson and the crew of The Beagle, plus Henri and Horatio.

Grubson Pug and his search party went to the Piazza San Marco which was a huge public square where people from the city and from ships liked to meet. Maybe Bonsai would be there?

They were astonished to find the Piazza crammed full of people, even early in the morning. Everyone was wearing fancy dress and masks and they were behaving quite strangely. They all seemed too excited – some were laughing in high-pitched voices but not at anything in particular. Some were silent – peering from behind masks in a very suspicious way. Some wore masks behind masks – and they were very mysterious! It was the one time in the year when everyone could leave their real lives to one side and romp around the city in a carefree way, being naughty and mischievous – because no one could recognise them anyway. What a day to look for a small white kitten!

Grubson suggested that they should split up and look around the huge square in two groups. This seemed like a faster way to cover more ground. Banzai, Sebastian

and Lefty set off to look in the huge cathedral whilst Grubson, Henri and Horatio decided to go somewhere as high up as possible to get a good view.

The campanile is a very tall bell tower at one end of the square. The tallest tower in Venice, it would give them a bird's eye view! Horatio made quite short work of the very steep staircase – after all, he lived at the top of eight flights of stairs at home, so he was used to the climb. It took Grubson and Henri quite a lot longer and they were both wheezing by the time they got to the top and stepped out onto the cold draughty roof of the campanile.

What a view they were treated to! They could see the Grand Canal and the lagoon and over to the island of San Michele where Grandfather now rested. Flags were flying over the rooftops and they could see The Beagle and The Resolve moored at the jetty. On such a clear morning they could even see the snowy peaks of the Alps in the far away distance.

Looking down they could see the mass of carnival-goers swirling around and dancing to the musicians in the square. There were ladies with tall powdered wigs, wearing huge flouncy dresses and hiding behind painted masks. And gentlemen with tricorn hats, wearing huge embroidered jackets and long lacy cuffs. There were quite a few dressed up in mysterious hooded cloaks like medieval monks. But the most spooky characters were those wearing big beaky masks.

"Everyone looks so tiny from up here," panted Henri. He was on tiptoe leaning over the edge of the campanile, desperately scanning the crowd for signs of a kitten. "Look how small that beaky monk looks – and the ladies' wigs which are really huge look quite small from all the way up here."

Grubson leaned over and tried to focus. Indeed everyone looked small from such a high tower, maybe this hadn't been such a good idea. But then he saw someone he recognised.

"Look!" exclaimed Grubson. "Look at Banzai down there. He really looks teeny weeney, doesn't he?"

Horatio and Henri followed Grubson's pointing paw and saw Banzai who stood out from the crowd because he was wearing a red bandana and no flouncy dress or cloak or mask. From this height he looked very small. He looked uncannily small in fact.

Realisation dawned on them.

"That's not Banzai!" said Horatio Fox quietly.

"That's Bonsai!" shouted Henri.

The three of them lost no time and sprinted down and round and down and round and down and round and down and round and down the hundreds of steps until they rushed out into the square below.

By this time of course, Bonsai was nowhere to be seen.

"Well," said Horatio optimistically. "At least we know he's here in Venice!"

They set off down a narrow cobbled street to continue the search.

Chapter Twelve

The Rialto Bridge

C aptain Dogmael, Tom and the crew were on the Rialto Bridge. Like everywhere else in the city, it was crowded with masked figures, laughing and dancing as their shrieking and singing got louder and more playful with every glass of wine. Constantly jostled by the crowds, Dogmael and his crew found it almost impossible not to lose one another, let alone find a small kitten.

Tom was finding it all quite upsetting. He didn't like the push and shove of the loud people and his legs were getting very tired. Instructing the rest of his crew to continue the search, Captain Dogmael carried his old cat to the side of the bridge where there was a little more room and they sat on the wall to catch their breath.

Despite the cold wind, they rested on the bridge licking ice creams. Quite befuddled by the antics of the Venice Carnival, their eyes were drawn to the Grand Canal beneath them. Almost as packed as the narrow streets, it was full of gondoliers transporting cats dressed as dogs and dogs dressed as cats to parties and palaces throughout the city.

"Life is so confusing sometimes," said Tom.

Dogmael was just about to agree with him when he spotted a small version of Banzai in a gondola heading straight down the Grand Canal towards them!

"Bonsai!" he shouted.

"Bonsai!" he called again.

"BONSAI!" they both shouted. Tom seemed to have regained his energy and joined in with Dogmael's frantic waving and shouting to the gondola below.

Bonsai looked up from his velvet gilded chair. He didn't recognise the dog or the cat on the bridge who seemed to know his name. He was a bit frightened and asked the gondolier to go faster to get away from them.

Unfortunately, the gondolier hadn't seen Nautilus that day and so he didn't know about the search for Bonsai. Instead he picked up speed and quickly guided his gondola underneath the bridge and on up the Grand Canal.

Tom and Dogmael jumped down from the wall, letting their ice creams fall into the water below. They struggled to cross the bridge, forcing their way across the tide of costumed revellers. By the time they got to the other side, they could just see the back of Bonsai's tiny head wearing a red bandana and disappearing up the Grand Canal in a speeding gondola.

Meanwhile, Sebastian and Lefty had lost Banzai in the crowds at San Marco but they had bumped into Nautilus and were travelling in his gondola through the narrow canals off the main routes. They were both wearing Carnival costumes – partly because Sebastian really liked the idea of dressing-up and mainly because Nautilus had insisted on it.

Sebastian was wearing a huge dress and a cat mask, whilst Lefty wore a cloak and hat with a beaky mask on his face. Perhaps not the best idea when they were meant to be helping to find Bonsai, but they were enjoying the Carnival atmosphere and it made Nautilus very happy to see them joining in.

They scoured the backwaters of Venice, around the labyrinth of narrow canals where there were fewer revellers. Their voices echoed around the tightly packed buildings as they called to Bonsai. Their unanswered voices sounded lonely and increasingly desperate and they started to lose hope of finding the little kitten. Even Nautilus stopped singing.

As they found themselves back on the Grand Canal and passing underneath the Rialto Bridge, Nautilus spotted Dogmael and Tom who were still slumped over the side. They were frustrated to have seen Bonsai, only for him to disappear.

"Why the long-a faces, eh?" called Nautilus from the water. "Eet is Carnevale and even though we must find the leetle kitty cat, we can still 'ave fun!" he called out jovially.

"Bonsai is in a gondola heading up the Grand Canal. He didn't stop because he didn't know us," called Dogmael to his friend.

He didn't recognise the passengers travelling with Nautilus and was quite shocked when Sebastian removed his cat mask and said, "We'll follow Bonsai whilst you try to find Banzai!" he suggested. "When Bonsai sees Banzai he'll know he's safe!"

"Good idea!" replied Dogmael. He struggled away towards San Marco through the flow of masks and wigs, slightly hampered by Tom who hobbled behind.

Nautilus heaved on his long pole.

"'Old on tight," he shouted to Sebastian and Lefty and they shot under the bridge and away.

Banzai's Unexpected Voyage

Chapter Thirteen

A Sign

Banzai had gone his own way when Sebastian and Lefty had started dressing up. He was far too worried about Bonsai to think about costumes and hats. Finding it hard to keep his spirits up, he wandered round and round and deeper into the maze of narrow alleyways and tiny bridges, aimlessly following his nose in the hope of finding some sign of Bonsai.

Turning a corner and finding yet another church and yet another tiny square with yet another well in the middle – he saw it. The sign!

It might have been quite easy to pass by without seeing it, but Banzai's sharp eyes were immediately drawn to something sparkly. Something white and knitted. Something white and knitted with sparkly silvery thread. Bonsai's Mr.Wong!

He must have been dropped as Bonsai scampered about looking for his uncle. Banzai scooped up the knitten and brushed off some dust. Mr.Wong looked a bit grubby and like he might have been trodden on a few times, but no lasting damage had been done.

Banzai perked up – this was a good sign! He started to run back towards San Marco where he had last seen Grubson. As he launched himself at full tilt down a narrow street he came nose to nose with Dogmael who had been running from the Rialto to look for him!

Panting to get his breath back, Dogmael explained where Bonsai had last been seen. Without another word, they turned tail and ran back towards the Grand Canal, looking in every gondola on the way – scattering glittery speckles through the air as they went.

By evening, the Carnival revellers were in full song. They had spent all day capering around the city having fun and they were well into their stride by nightfall.

Bonsai was hungry and tired and quite bamboozled by all the cats who looked like dogs and beaky monks and people calling to him from the bridge. And he had lost his knitten.

He felt like crying. *And I think he was allowed to – he was only three after all.*

His paws were sore from walking around Venice all day, his fur was damp from getting too close to the canals and his tummy was rumbling. He had seen too many strange and startling masks and too many times he had mistakenly followed a figure which looked like a white cat, only to find it was a dog in disguise. Confused and tired, he squished himself into a church doorway and fell asleep in the shadows, where no one would see him.

No one at all in fact.

All across Venice the search was called off and the two weary crews returned to their ships. They needed to rest before they could start looking for Bonsai again. Marjorie tutted and flapped as she dished up spaghetti for the hungry sailors. It wasn't easy for her as she kept getting the stringy pasta tangled around her feet and stuck to her beak. No one said very much around The Beagle table that evening. They were all very busy trying to control their spaghetti and very worried about the missing kitten.

Banzai was happy to be back on board The Beagle again but he felt quiet and slightly desperate that no-one had found his little nephew. He knew his sister Katinka must be very worried and he felt partly responsible, because Bonsai had heard stories of how he had run away to sea and had copied him. Kittens like to copy.

After dinner, Henri cleaned up Bonsai's knitten. He carefully washed the dust and dirt from the delicate little knitted face and body and dried it off before returning it to Banzai. He watched as the sad cat popped Bonsai's knitten into his carpet bag along with his own Mr.Wong.

Two Wongs, but nothing seemed right.

Henri knew he had to help Banzai again and went on deck to find Horatio Fox who was staring intently across the water towards a particularly magnificent building. Horatio explained to his little friend that this was the home of the mayor of Venice. The Doge of Venice to give him his official title. The Doge was a very kind Labrador (known to his friends as the Labradoge) and it was his job to make sure that everyone in Venice was happy. If people had problems, he tried to sort them out and Horatio thought he would be just the person to help in the search for Bonsai. Henri and Horatio hopped into a gondola and set off across the water.

Although it was now very late, the kindly old Doge listened as Henri explained the Bonsai problem. He reassured the worried pup that the citizens of Venice loved children and no harm would come to little Bonsai. He then had a chat with some of his advisers and said he would offer a reward to the person who brought Bonsai to him – one hundred golden ducats. That should work! He gave orders to have Reward posters printed overnight and stuck all over Venice by morning. With everyone in Venice looking for him, Bonsai would soon be found!

The Doge clapped his hands and was immediately attended by secretaries and messengers. An artist was called and a painting of Bonsai was made according to Henri's careful description of Banzai.

Shortly before midnight, the Doge's clerk, a long-aired Dachshund named Daniel, hurried out of a palace side-door and ran across town. He ran all the way to the home of the sleeping printer who jumped out of bed and (still wearing his nightshirt) immediately inked up his presses and set to work printing one thousand posters – by order of The Doge!

Chapter Fourteen

Cat Show at The Doge's Palace

The next morning, the citizens of Venice woke up bleary-eyed and slightly confused. All of them had spent the previous day and most of the night campering around the alleys and canals playing tricks and being tricked. The morning-after is always a slow time.

This particular morning-after was a little different however. All over the city every available wall, lamp-post and doorway was plastered with posters of the missing Bonsai's little worried face. By order of the Doge himself there was a one hundred golden ducat reward for anyone who could find him and bring him to the palace.

One hundred golden ducats as a reward for finding a little white kitten wearing a red polka dot bandana!

The Venetians forgot about bleary eyes and blurry memories of the night before. Frantic activity broke out across the watery city, as every white kitten suddenly became very popular. The air was filled with strange little kissing noises as kittens were tempted out from underneath beds, inside wardrobes and from up high on balconies. The tinkling sound of food bowls being tapped with spoons rang out through alleys, balls of wool were unravelled and toy mice were waggled across floors and into boxes to tempt and catch the unsuspecting kittens of Venice.

Every white kitten in the city was soon scooped from its favourite snoozing place and whisked indoors to be fitted with a bandana. Haberdashers and dressmakers ran out of red polka dot materials. Undeterred, pans of red dye were set to bubble in fireplaces as, thinking of one hundred golden ducats, the Venetians made their own bandanas to match the one on the poster.

The colouring didn't end there. No kitten was safe. When every white kitten had been found, claimed or stolen, the citizens set to work with the others. Black, tabby, and ginger kittens quickly found themselves being brushed with plumes of white wig powder left over from

Carnival. Soon every kitten in Venice was white. With a red polka dot bandana on its head.

The first kitten arrived at the Doge's Palace shortly after nine o'clock with a smiley faced owner already planning how to spend the one hundred golden ducats.

By a quarter past nine, there were thirty-seven white kittens at the Doge's Palace.

By half past ten there were seventy-eight white kittens – all of them wearing bandanas.

Confusion reigned within the palace walls and the anxious Doge didn't know which way to turn. He usually rattled around in the vast empty spaces of his palace feeling quite lonely. Now he felt overcrowded and the noisy kittens hurt his sensitive old ears. Room after room was opened up to make space for all the kittens and their owners. The palace officials left their meeting rooms and private chambers to help provide bowls of water and biscuits to keep their little furry visitors happy. Outside, kittens kept arriving and the Doge started to panic.

What had he got into? Which one was Bonsai? What was he going to do?

Whilst all this was going on, across the city in the quietness of Campo San Antonio, a small sleepy kitten, undiscovered and hidden in the shadows of a church doorway, woke up from a deep sleep. He yawned widely, stretched his back legs one at a time, licked his tail smooth and straightened his bandana. Rubbing his rumbling tummy he stared bleakly at the empty square.

Bonsai wondered why the canals and alleys were so quiet and empty and he wondered where he had dropped his knitten.

"Mr.Wong!" he cried to himself.

He had never felt more alone. Or hungry.

Just then the church door creaked open and a long nose poked out – whiskers twitching in the fresh air and beady eyes blinking in the bright February sunshine. Nautilus!

Nautilus had been inside the church all night, praying to San Antonio for the safe discovery of Bonsai. He had tried so hard to find him the previous day and he hoped the patron saint of lost things (including kittens) might help in the search. More than anything, he knew how frightened a tiny little kitten from a foreign land must be if he was lost in Venice. Desperately hoping for help from on high, Nautilus had lit candles for San Antonio and had murmured prayers through the night in the empty echoing church.

He was tired after searching and praying through the night and his knees hurt from all that kneeling. Surely he deserved a miracle! Leaving the church, he almost tripped over Bonsai who was still on the step staring up at him, waiting to see who was on the end of the long whiskery nose.

"Holy San Antonio and all the saints … can it be … is it?" mumbled Nautilus. He pulled himself together and said to Bonsai, "Your Uncle Banzai asked me to look for you, little Bonsai. If you come with me I'll take you to him and then get you something to eat."

At the thought of Banzai and breakfast Bonsai perked up and purred very loudly. He snuggled up to Nautilus and gripped on to his sore knobbly knees.

"It's a meeeeeeeeeerickle," screamed Nautilus clicking his heels as he and Bonsai scampered across the square and away to the canal and his waiting gondola. "Holy St.Tony – it's a meeeeerickle!"

Cat Show at The Doge's Palace

Inside the Doge's palace, there was mayhem. By this time there were ninety-two white kittens, all of them wearing red polka dot bandanas. Horatio and Henri tried to comfort the Doge who was starting to flap at the situation. They looked at one another nervously; they wished Banzai would hurry up and get to the palace but even then, how would he recognise Bonsai? He'd never met him before!

Outside the Doge's Palace, Daniel gripped his clipboard a little bit tighter and sighed with frustration when he saw Nautilus approaching with yet another white kitten wearing a red polka dot bandana.

"Ciao, signor," said Nautilus cheerily. "I've-a brought the Bonsai to meet 'is Uncle Banzai. I think he's 'ere at the palace."

"Sure you 'ave. Everyone is a-bringing Bonsai to meet 'is Uncle Banzai 'ere at the Doge's Palace. Why not, eh? I gotta nothing better to do anyway eh? 'undreds and 'undreds of leetle white kittens eh? The Doge – he make a beeg mistake this-a time." Daniel was very agitated.

Nautilus and Bonsai looked at one another in puzzlement. They had seen the posters on their way here and had been expecting a warm welcome from the Doge himself.

" 'Ere is your number. Steeck it on your bandana and go inside. Take a place – eef you can-a find space," Daniel mumbled, unaware that he was looking at the real Bonsai.

Nautilus and Bonsai hurried inside the palace and trotted along the marble colonnades towards the inner courtyard and the giant staircase as directed by Daniel. As they got closer they could hear the muffled sound of meowing and purring with some hissing mixed in. The noise grew louder and louder and when they turned the final corner into the courtyard, it was almost deafening. They froze in their footsteps as they stared at rows and rows and rows of white kittens – all the way up the staircase and all of them wearing red bandanas.

Just then the Doge stood up and asked for quiet. Bonsai could see a tall fox and a small French Pug standing next to him. Doing as he was told, Bonsai took a place near the back and listened as the Doge made his next mistake.

"Which one of you is Bonsai?" the Doge asked the assembled kittens.

"MEEEEEEEEEEEEEEEEEEEEEEEEEEEEEEEEEEEE EEEEEEEEEEEEEEEEEEEEEEEEEEEEEEEEEEEEEE – ow," screaked ninety-three white kittens.

The screeching got louder and higher pitched with every collective screak from the kittens.

"MEEEEEEEEEEEEEEEEEEEEEEEEEEEEEEEEE EEEEEEEEEEEEEEEEEEEEEEEEEEEEEEEE- ow."

The Doge was sweating and trembling as he ordered them, then begged them, to stop the caterwauling. Turning to Horatio he raised an eyebrow and said, "Now what eh? This ees a catastrophe!"

Horatio and Henri were perplexed. They had not expected this. They had expected perhaps two or three kittens to come to the Doge in cases of mistaken identity, but not this! They looked at the mass of white kittens helplessly – they all sort of looked like Banzai and there were so many of them that they got a kind of snow blindness from all the white fur.

The Doge, Horatio and Henri stepped outside the palace to give their ears a rest and to get a good idea. They didn't get one. Not a single idea, never mind a good one. Henri gave a bark of relief when he saw the familiar figure of Banzai sauntering across the piazza towards them, swinging his nice light carpet bag as he came. Daniel, still clutching his clipboard, bowed deeply to the flustered Doge and ran across the square to meet him.

"Permezzo signor," he said, fixing Banzai with a stern look. "Please – to come with me straightaway – subito – immediately!" Poor Daniel could hardly take any more stress and he was desperate for Banzai to come and choose a kitten and then everyone could go home and leave him and the Labradoge in peace!

"Prepare yourself" he whispered to the startled Banzai as he pushed backwards against the double doors and twirled into the palace courtyard with Banzai close behind.

Ninety-three white kittens saw a bigger version of themselves enter the chamber and as one, took a deep breath and screamed

"Uncle Baaaaaaanzzzaaaaaaaaaiiiiiiiiiiiiiiiiiiiiiii!"

"UNCLE BAAAAAAAAAAAAANZZZZAAAAAAA AAAAAIIIIIIIIIIII!"

Banzai could hear the Doge whimpering behind him and Henri let out a small squeak. But Banzai knew how to handle kittens. Calmly, he raised a paw to his mouth and pressed his lips together. The ninety-three kittens all did the same. Kittens like to copy. Copy-cats.

Silence.

Even Daniel was impressed.

Lifting his carpet bag, Banzai quietly cranked it open and dipped his arm inside.

Wordlessly he pulled out Bonsai's knitten and held it up for all to see, the sparkles glittering in the shafts of sunlight coming in through arches and colonnades.

Ninety-two pairs of kitten eyes looked at the knitten blankly.

One little voice shouted from the back row, quite clearly.

"Mr.Wong!"

Chapter Fifteen

Ciao (Meow)

Over the next couple of days, life returned to normal in Venice and kittens of all colours reappeared in alleyways, up on rooftops and underneath beds. Captain Grubson and Captain Dogmael were busy with the merchants of Venice, buying and selling. They filled the holds of their ships with spices and silks, glasses and vases, furniture and paintings, wine and olives.

On board The Beagle, Sebastian was busy inspecting the stitching on the sails and Lefty was double-checking all the ropes and rigging and knots. There was a long voyage ahead of them and they needed to make sure everything was ship-shape.

Marjorie had a wonderful time in the market. She stocked up the galley with pasta and tomatoes, cheeses, herbs and garlic (Banzai was pleased).

The crew on board The Resolve were busy too and this included Tom! He had come out of his brief retirement for the voyage back home to St Benfro and was up in his crow's nest tightening rivets and twiddling with his telescope. It had taken him almost an hour to get up there and no one could bear to watch his slow and rickety climb, expecting him to plummet to the deck at every minute. He was excited to be making one last voyage home to St Benfro before finally retiring from his life at sea.

Banzai and Bonsai were both high up in the crow's nest on The Beagle. Bonsai was to be Banzai's apprentice to learn all about being a ship's cat before joining Dogmael's crew: when Tom retired, The Resolve would be in need of a good ship's cat. Bonsai copied everything Banzai did. When Banzai swabbed the deck

– Bonsai swabbed the deck. When Banzai polished the brasses – Bonsai polished the brasses. When Banzai stopped for a sip of water – Bonsai sipped water too. When Banzai mopped his brow – Bonsai mopped his. When Banzai whistled, Bonsai whistled. When Banzai chewed garlic, Bonsai chewed too.

On the second afternoon, just before sailing home, Banzai and Bonsai were in the crow's nest doing telescope practice. Bonsai was viewing Venice through a rolled up map when he spotted his hero, Nautilus, leaning against a lamp-post looking very dejected. This was most unlike Nautilus! Happy, smiling, always-jolly Nautilus?

Banzai called to the water-rat to join them all on board the deck of The Beagle where Marjorie was just serving hot chocolate to warm everyone up in the cold February sunshine.

Once they were settled, Grubson asked Nautilus what was wrong.

The water rat took a deep breath, rubbed his tummy and puffed out again.

"The Doge," he said. "The Doge 'e gave me one hundred golden ducats. For finding Bonsai." He rolled his eyes and sighed loudly again.

No one quite understood why this was a problem.

"The theeng-a eees," said Nautilus musically, "I didn't really find eem. I nearly tripped over 'eem. I 'ad been praying for 'eem to San Antonio. But it was miracle what found 'eem, eh? A miraculous big meeeeerickle. San Antonio found 'eem and popped 'eem just outside the church door for me to trip over. I don't deserve the one hundred golden ducats."

"You could take it anyway?" suggested Horatio. "It might be very useful for you one day."

"No, holy St.Tony. Finder of kittens!" exclaimed Nautilus. "I am 'appy now – 'ow I am, eh? I live 'ere in this wonderful watery city with my bellissima laydee wife and all my water rat family and friends and cousins and uncles and aunties and nieces and nephews and we are all gondoliers – we are singing gondoliers and we are 'appy. Money might change us. Money might make us un'appy eh?"

No one could think of what to say. Until Bonsai spoke up.

"You are very lucky Nautilus," he said. "You have all your big family and your nephews and friends and I can't remember them all – but you are all together and happy. When I was lost and hungry and hiding and looking, I didn't know anyone and was all alone. I was very frightened. I even lost my knitten – so I didn't have any friends at all. And everyone needs a Mr.Wong. Everyone needs a friend."

Nautilus stared at the little white kitten. His whiskers twitched and his eyes got rounder. Suddenly he opened his mouth.

"That's eeet! Holy Santa Maria della Salute – of course!" shouted the exuberant Nautilus, quite back to his old bouncing beaming self again.

"Come with me my leetle friend – just-a one more thing to do before you sail away! We just 'ave time if we 'urry."

Bonsai and Nautilus jumped into his gondola and shot away up the canal. Grubson watched them go with a slight sinking feeling. He didn't like it when his ship's cats kept running off.

Across the city, in a quiet little square overshadowed by the lesser-known church of San Antonio, the kindly Brother Bernard was feeding some stray kittens. Every day he used the few coins he had to buy food and milk to help the lost and lonely. Brother

Bernard was a huge, very furry monk with a gentle nature and he spent his life rescuing anyone who was a lost kitten. The tiny strays loved and trusted him and always knew that they would have a safe place to sleep in the church of San Antonio.

But Brother Bernard was worried. The collection plate was sometimes half empty and he knew he couldn't afford to keep feeding and rescuing the lost kittens of Venice. How would he ever be able to turn them away into the cold weather with empty tummies?

As he fed the mass of kittens who were hurriedly noshing their scraps of food, Brother Bernard heard an excited shout from across the square. Nautilus and Bonsai were running towards him smiling and pointing to the bag of coins which Nautilus was carrying above his head.

The kindly monk held out his arms in greeting and pumped water from the central well to give them each a drink whilst they caught their breath. When they had finished drinking, Nautilus wiped his mouth with the back of his paw and fixed Brother Bernard with a serious expression.

"I 'ave come to save San Antonio," he announced.

Brother Bernard was confused but smiled as he said, "This is very kind of you Signor Nautilus. But San

Antonio is the saviour – the saver of little lost kittens. Even though my church of San Antonio is very poor and may not be able to stay open much longer, how can you save us?"

Nautilus breathlessly explained the story.

"Eet ees a meeeerickle, Brother Bernard," he said solemnly. "San Antonio helped me to find Bonsai. Then the wonderful Doge – our most loved and bellisimo Labradoge – 'e gave me one hundred golden ducats! But it wasn't me! It was San Antonio! It was San Antonio and you who save so many leetle kitty cats. And you is so poor and I don't need-a the money . . . so eet ees for you and San Antonio and all the lost kittens."

Brother Bernard gulped at the kindness of Nautilus as he accepted the bag of money. He hugged the excited water rat and stroked Bonsai's head as he quietly thanked San Antonio for the second miracle in two days!

"Thank you signor," he said. "Thank you for saving the church of San Antonio so that we can continue to rescue any lost and hungry kittens who need our help. This money will last us for a very long time. You are an angel sent to help us all!"

Nautilus blushed and said that he thought Brother Bernard might be right.

Watching Venice slip away from them, Banzai and Bonsai were very sad to go. They waved from the crow's nest and bowed their heads as The Beagle sailed slowly past the island of San Michele. Grandfather's mimosa tree would soon be covered in fragrant orange flowers, where he had a view of the sea all around and he would never ever get wet.

"Goodbye Grandfather," called Banzai. He knew he had done exactly the right thing for his fussy old Grandpapa.

On the deck, Horatio and Henri were waving to the Doge and Daniel who stood outside their pretty palace and waved to the departing ships.

"Come back to us soon" called the friendly old Labrador who was much happier now that his ears had stopped ringing. Daniel glanced up at him and smiled bravely.

"Oh Papa," sighed Henri. "I hope we can return to Venice soon. It is a magical place and I will miss everyone. Especially Nautilus."

No sooner had the words left Henri's mouth than they heard a cheery shout from behind them. A flotilla of gondolas was following the ships to the mouth of the lagoon – led by Nautilus who was singing and shouting as usual!

"Ciao, my friends – goodbye! Come back soon – don't-a be sad! Remember – in Italian, it is the same word for goodbye and hello! Ciao! Goodbye! Hello!"

So The Beagle and The Resolve pointed west and sailed away towards St Benfro and home. The crews on both ships waved until they could no longer hear the gondoliers and Venice seemed to flatten into a mirage on the horizon – as if it had been a beautiful dream and nothing more.

Banzai's Unexpected Voyage

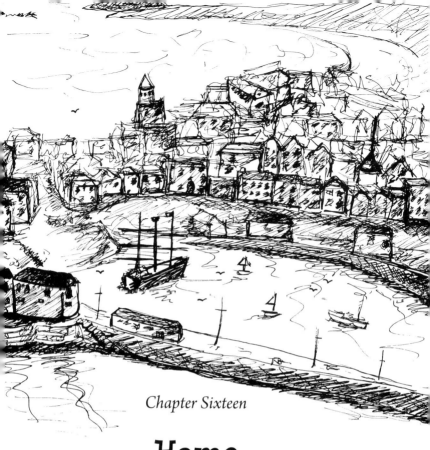

Chapter Sixteen

Home

W hen The Beagle and The Resolve arrived home to St Benfro it was already the third week of March. Spring had arrived. Wild flowers decorated the headlands surrounding the harbour town which was now yellow with daffodils in every garden, basket and window box.

Henri was excited. He had made his first ever voyage on The Beagle and all his navigation and chart mapping lessons had paid off. He knew that one day he would become the next Captain Grubson to sail the world on The Beagle, just like his papa. He had missed his brother and sisters and was looking forward to seeing them. And he was quite overcome with his mama's pride when he ran down the gangplank and jumped into her waiting arms! She had never believed he would be strong enough or brave enough to become a sailor and how wrong she had been!

The Grubson children were intrigued to meet the tiny Bonsai. He was a little white shadow to his Uncle Banzai as he followed him down the gangplank, each of them carrying a carpet bag.

"Now remember what I told you Bonsai," said Banzai. "Coins and telescopes, garlic and spare bandanas might fill up your carpet bag but they will not weigh you down like guilt. Just make sure you keep your promises, no matter how difficult. Keep up with your reading and writing and then you won't go wrong."

That evening (and into the night) the landlord and his wife were delighted as everyone crammed into The Three Buccaneers to hear the stories of what had happened on Banzai's unexpected voyage. Much later – well after midnight, when the stories had been told, and questions had been answered, everyone went home to their beds and hammocks. Only two of us remained in the pub. We were both writing by the light of the fire embers. I was writing my hurried notes for this story. My companion was writing a scratchy letter on tissue-thin paper – to his mother, to let her know that he and his nephew Bonsai were both safely in St Benfro.

But the story doesn't quite end there…

Over the next few weeks, several ships arrived in St Benfro bringing some unexpected cargo. The first to arrive was a grand piano from London addressed to:

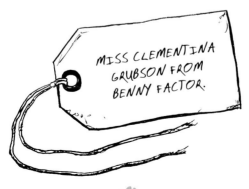

MISS CLEMENTINA GRUBSON FROM BENNY FACTOR.

Surprised and completely mystified about who Benny Factor might be, Clementina was delighted with her beautiful gift. After months of practice, she had become a very good pianist and she was able to play the most enchanting music on this very special grand piano.

The next mystery gift was labelled:

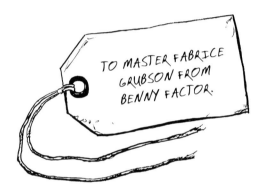

TO MASTER FABRICE GRUBSON FROM BENNY FACTOR.

Excited to receive an unexpected gift, Fabrice needed help from his father to unpack the shiny, proper, professional twenty-one gear racing bike! It had been sent from St Malo. Grubson had his suspicions about which shop this may have come from, but he had no idea about the real identity of Benny Factor. Fabrice jumped on to his gleaming new bicycle and whizzed off up the hill, full of excitement for next year's Tour de St Benfro Race. He already had his eyes on the gold medal!

Bella had said nothing when her siblings had received such wonderful presents. She had learned not to be jealous about the good fortune of others. However, she could hardly contain herself when another crate arrived at the Grubson household. It had been sent from Seville with a label attached:

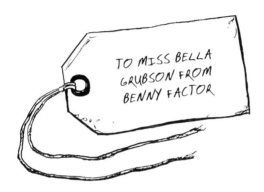

TO MISS BELLA GRUBSON FROM BENNY FACTOR

Inside, she found six party dresses made of the finest satin and silk with lacy bits and bows. They were the colours of jewels and glittered with sequins. Bella, for once, was speechless with joy. When she tried on each dress and smilingly showed them to her papa without preening and asking for compliments, Grubson genuinely thought she had never looked prettier.

Grubson was very suspicious now. These were all exactly the Christmas presents which had been ruined and lost in the storm off Monastery Island in December. Who was the mystery benefactor? None of the crew seemed to know. Marjorie, who usually knew everything, was just as puzzled as everyone else.

But Grubson was even more confused when a fourth parcel arrived at the Grubson house. He thought that all the presents which had been lost at sea had now been mysteriously and magically replaced. What was this? This one was tiny with a huge label attached:

TO CAPTIN GRUBSON PUG OF THE BEAGLE.

IN A STORM
LIVES WOZ SAVED
BUT PRESINTS WOZ LOST
AND CRISTMAS DAY WOZ GAPPY.
THE CAPTIN WOZ SAD
BUT IT WOZN'T THAT BAD
HE WOZ HOME SO HIS CHILDEREN WOZ HAPPY.

ALL ALLONE
FAR AWAY
A KITTEN WOZ LOST
AND KARNIVAL WOZ SPOOKY.
THERE WOZ A BIG SURCH
HE WOZ FOWND NEAR A CHURCH
BUT THE MIRACKLE WOZ A BIT FLUKEY.
(HIS KNITTEN WOZ LOST AS WELL BUT WE
FOWND THAT).

IN A BAG
FULL OF SEACRETS
THIS SHIP WOZ LOST
SO I THORT I'D SEND IT TO YOU.
IT LOOKS LIKE YOUR BOAT
SO I'M SENDING THIS NOAT
COZ ST ANTHONY HASN'T A CLUE.

Grubson knew at once what was inside the tiny parcel.

He put all the mysteries together and they suddenly made sense.

The repeat voyage to London, St Malo and Seville.

Replacement Christmas presents that only very few people would have known about.

A cat who unexpectedly vanished from St Benfro with a heavy bag and came back with a light one.

The inventive spelling on the labels.

An unknown benefactor.

And the little golden brooch he had bought for Adele – and had hidden in Banzai's bag during the Christmas storm – where it had been forgotten … of course!

Without unwrapping the tiny box, Grubson gave the parcel to his wife.

"This is your Christmas present Adele," he said. "I thought it had been lost during the shipwreck, but it seems that every lost thing eventually returns to its rightful owner. And this has come home to you."

Mrs Grubson quickly tore off the paper and opened the small velvet box. Inside was a brooch. A small golden brooch in the shape of a ship in full sail – just like the Beagle. It was made of delicately engraved gold and a diamond flashed at the top of the mast.

"I will wear this every time you are away on a voyage, Grubson," she said, smiling. "That way I know that The Beagle and you will never be lost and will always come home safely."

That evening, when Banzai had finished arm-wrestling in The Three Buccaneers, Grubson bought his little furry friend a drink and they sat by the fire talking about Venice.

Turning to his beloved cat, Grubson asked, "So Banzai. Did you finally manage to empty everything out of that heavy old carpet bag of yours?"

"Yessssssss," smiled Banzai, breathing out a relieved sigh. "In fact, it was only a couple of days ago when I was giving it a spring clean that I found the very last object in there – which shouldn't have been in there at all."

"I think that little golden ship is now safely in the right place at last," said Grubson, winking at Banzai.

"Everything which is lost eventually returns home or finds a new place to belong. With a little help, they all find their way in the end, whether they're tiny golden brooches hidden in a storm, grandfathers who can't find the right place to rest or little white kittens lost in Venice. They all find their way home – just like you."

The End

Thank you!

Thank you to all the children who asked me to write this book – all of you desperate to know what Banzai keeps in his carpet bag. There were some good guesses, but I think Banzai surprised us all!

Thank you – to Caroline Smailes for being such a wonderful reader and editor, and for your generosity of spirit.

Thank you – to Matt for the sailing expertise when calculating the length of time a voyage to Venice might take a galleon crewed by dogs and cats!

And, as ever – thank YOU for reading this book. Stories need readers as much as they need writers – your feedback and enthusiasm are very much appreciated. By the way – did anyone spot the small (and slightly desperate) puppy wearing a cat mask at the Doge's Palace? Not strictly a part of the story – but a surprise addition from Sam!

More from Whistling Cat Books.

Banzai's Unexpected Voyage is the sequel to Grubson Pug's Christmas Voyage.

GRUBSON PUG'S CHRISTMAS VOYAGE

How far will Captain Grubson go to make this Christmas special?

Grubson Pug, his crew of dogs, an arm-wrestling Siamese cat called Banzai and Marjorie the parrot set sail from St Benfro somewhere in the west of Wales, in search of Christmas presents for his demanding children.

Desperate to hurry home by Christmas Eve, they run into fierce winter storms and Grubson has some big decisions to make.

"Grubson Pug (a dog without a gram of pugnaciousness in his body) is faced with a Christmas list that would give anyone a headache. But then – he's an adventurous, old-fashioned seadog, and above all, a family dog, so he sets out on a voyage to find something that will suit everybody. As you can guess, it's not exactly plain sailing... So stoke up the fire, draw the curtains, gather everyone together, jump on the sofa, switch on the reading lamp and enjoy this charming little heart-warmer together."
Ian Whybrow (author of Little Wolf series)

Primary Times Christmas Books recommendation.

Rubery Book Award longlisted 2013.

To buy the books and for competitions and activities, please visit
www.whistlingcatbooks.com